A Book of Dragons

*by the same author
and artist*

A BOOK OF GIANTS

A BOOK OF DWARFS

A BOOK OF DRAGONS

Ruth Manning-Sanders
DRAWINGS BY
Robin Jacques

E. P. Dutton & Co., Inc.,   New York

First published in the U.S.A., 1965 by E. P. Dutton & Co., Inc.

Copyright, ©, 1964 by Ruth Manning-Sanders
All rights reserved. Printed in the U.S.A.

FIRST EDITION

Library of Congress Catalog Card Number: 65-19578

Foreword

Not all dragons want to gobble up princesses. Some of them are kindly beasts, like the dragon in *Pepito*, and *The Dragon of the Well* – two stories which come from Greece. And some dragons are proud beings who serve the Supreme Ruler of Heaven, and control the weather – you can see them sometimes in the sky on a cloudy day. Such are the Chinese dragons in the stories *Chien Tang*, and *The Yellow Dragon*, and *Baskets in a Little Cart*. And such is the Japanese dragon in *My Lord Bag of Rice*.

But there are also, of course, bad and savage dragons, who have to be either killed or outwitted. These you will find in the Macedonian story, *Yanni*; in the Irish story, *The Thirteenth Son*; in the Rumanian story, *Stan Bolovan*; in the two Greek stories, *The Nine Doves*, and *Constantes*; in the two German stories, *The Three Dogs*, and *The Dragon and his Grandmother*; and in the Slav story, *The Prince with the Golden Hand*.

Probably the one dragon that everybody has heard of is the dragon that St George conquered. The legend tells that this dragon lived in a pond outside the town of Silene in Libya; and unless he was given plenty of sheep to eat, he would come out of his pond, prance up to the town walls, and kill the townsfolk with his poisonous breath. When the people of Silene ran out of sheep, they took to offering their daughters to the dragon. The girls were chosen by lot, and one day the lot fell to the king's daughter. The dragon was just scrambling out of his pond to devour her, when a

5

Christian knight called George came riding by. Making the sign of the cross, he charged the dragon with his lance, and it fell to the ground. George then told the princess to tie her girdle round this much disheartened dragon, and lead it to the town, which she did.

By this miracle the king and all the citizens were converted to Christianity. But, later, George was tortured and put to death by the heathen emperor, Diocletian. So he became *Saint* George the Martyr, and was idolized in many eastern countries. And when the Crusaders returned from the East, they brought back with them such glowing stories of St George's valour and piety, that he was chosen as the patron saint of England.

But you will not find *St George and the Dragon* among the stories in this book; because this is a book of fairy tales, and the story of St George belongs more properly to legend.

Contents

1· Constantes and the Dragon

There were three brothers, and the youngest was called Constantes. And these brothers went to look for work. Soon they came near to a mountain, and under the mountain was a cornfield. The corn was ripe, and ready for cutting.

Said Constantes, 'Let us reap this corn; and when the owner comes, he will pay us.'

So they began to reap the corn.

And, as they were reaping, the mountain trembled, and out from it leaped a dragon.

Said Constantes, 'Here comes the owner of the cornfield!'

The dragon had only small wings, but he was moving very fast, half hopping and half flying. He gave a jump down into the cornfield, and said, 'What are you doing?'

Said Constantes, 'We are reaping your corn, in the hope that you will pay us.'

Said the dragon, 'Reap on.'

So they reaped on. And when the corn was half of it reaped, the dragon said to Constantes, 'Go to that mountain and give this letter to my wife.'

Constantes took the letter, and went to the mountain. And when he was out of sight of the dragon, he opened the letter and read it. The letter said:

The man I am sending to you, kill him and put him in the

9

oven and cook him. And have him ready for my supper when I come home.

But Constantes tore the letter into little pieces, and hid the pieces under a stone. And he wrote another letter. And this was what he wrote:

My dear Dragoness,

When the bearer of this letter arrives, I beg you to kill the best turkey, and stuff it and roast it. Also fill a basket full of loaves, and send him back here with food for my labourers.

So the dragoness did all that. And Constantes carried the loaves and the roast turkey to the cornfield.

When the dragon saw him, he thought, 'Ah, that lad is a cleverer rogue than I!'

And when the three lads had finished the reaping, the dragon said, 'Come home with me now, for your supper and your pay.'

And they went with the dragon, and he gave them their supper, but not their pay. He said, 'Stay the night here. You shall have your pay in the morning.'

So the lads went to bed.

Said Constantes, 'There is some trick about this. We must keep awake!' But his brothers went to sleep. Only Constantes stayed awake.

The dragon and the dragoness went to bed, and they were talking. And Constantes heard what they said.

Said the dragon, 'First thing in the morning, I will kill those lads, and you shall cook them for my breakfast.'

Said the dragoness, 'That I will!'

And they yawned, and slept.

And Constantes rose up, and went into their room, and saw them sleeping. And he drew the ring off the finger of the dragoness, and went back to his brothers, and shook them. Said he to his brothers,

'Wake, boys, wake! The dragon will kill us first thing in the morning!'

So they rose up from their beds and ran off.

In the morning, the dragon rose up and went into the lads' room, thinking to kill them. And the dragoness woke up and shouted, 'Dragon, my ring has gone!'

And the dragon shouted back, 'The lads have gone too!'

And he bounded out of the house and pursued them.

He saw them in the distance, running, and shouted, 'Stop, lads, stop! I must pay you your wages!'

And Constantes shouted back over his shoulder, 'We want no wages.'

And they ran on.

The dragon shouted, 'Come back, dear lads, come back!'

But they made no answer, they fled on, and came to a city. And the dragon turned back and went home. For he might not enter the king's city.

The three lads took service with the king; but Constantes was quicker at his work, and cleverer than his brothers. And the king showed him favour. And the brothers were jealous.

And the eldest brother went to the king, and said, 'Constantes has the ring of the dragoness, and he wears it on his middle finger. It is a ring like no other on earth. Only a king should wear that ring. But Constantes will give it up to no man.'

So the king sent for Constantes and said, 'Let me see the ring that you wear on your middle finger.' And Constantes took the ring off his finger and showed it to the king. And it sparkled.

Said the king, 'It is a ring for a king to wear.'

Said Constantes, 'It is yours, my liege.' And he gave it to the king. So he became more in favour than before; and the king gave him a new suit of clothes.

But the eldest brother went to the king again, and said, 'The dragon has a diamond-spangled counterpane. Such a counterpane should be on a king's bed.'

Said the king, 'But how to get it?'

Said the eldest brother, 'Constantes boasts daily that he can get it.'

So the king sent for Constantes and said, 'Get me the dragon's diamond-spangled counterpane.'

Said Constantes, 'I cannot get it.'

Then the king grew angry and said, 'What! Have you not been boasting daily that you could get it? Bring it to me, or I will have your head!'

And Constantes went out of the city, not knowing what he should do.

And in a vineyard he met an old woman, who said, 'Whither away, Constantes?'

Said Constantes, 'Whither away, indeed! I do not know whither away. The king bids me bring him the diamond-spangled counterpane of the dragon, or he will have my head. I cannot get that counterpane.'

Said the old woman, 'You can get it! Go back to the king.'

And she told him what to ask for, and what to do.

So Constantes went to the king and asked for a reed full of fleas. He took the reed full of fleas and went to the dragon's house. By the time he got there, it was night, and the dragons were in bed. And Constantes climbed up the wall outside the dragons' bedroom, and pulled out two bricks to make a hole. And he put the reed through the hole, and shook the fleas out of the reed on to the counterpane.

The fleas bit the dragon on the face and neck, and the dragon woke up and shouted, 'A curse on this counterpane, it is full of fleas!' And he threw the counterpane out of the window. And Constantes picked it up and ran with it back towards the city.

He was all night running, for it was a long way. At dawn the dragon woke, and said, 'Get up, dragoness. Go down and give that counterpane a good shake, and bring it up to me again. I'm feeling chilly.'

The dragoness went downstairs and came running up again, crying out, 'Dragon, your counterpane has gone!'

The dragon bounced out of bed and looked through the window. Far away, over the fields and through the vineyards, he saw something moving, and glittering in the first rays of the sun. Constantes had the diamond-spangled counterpane on his back, and it quite covered him up, but the dragon could see his feet running.

'It's that Constantes!' he shouted. And he rushed out of the house and gave chase, bawling, 'Give me that counterpane! What trick have you been playing, you dog?'

And Constantes shouted back over his shoulder. 'What I have done so far is nothing. Wait and see what I shall do to you soon!'

And he got into the city, and the dragon had to turn back.

Then Constantes gave the diamond-spangled counterpane to the king. He became more in favour than he was before. And the king gave him two new suits of clothes.

But the eldest brother raged in his heart, and went to the king and said, 'The dragon has a silver horse, and a golden bell with forty-one holes in it to let out the music. Constantes boasts daily that he will get the silver horse and the golden bell for himself; he boasts that he will ride round the town on the silver horse, whilst the golden bell lets out its music. And he boasts that the people will say, "Look! There goes one finer than the king himself!"'

And the king was angry, and sent for Constantes, and said, 'What, fellow! Are you setting yourself up to be finer than I am? Bring me that golden bell and that silver horse, that I may ride on it myself. If you do not bring it, you shall lose your head.'

13

Constantes went out of the city, and there in the vineyard he met the old woman. And she said to him, 'Whither away this time, Constantes?'

Constantes answered, 'Nay, I know not.' He told the old woman what he was ordered to do, and the old woman told him how he should do it.

So Constantes made forty-one wooden plugs, and bought three pounds of barley sugar, and set out with the plugs and the barley sugar for the dragon's house. When he got there it was night, and he went into the stable; and the silver horse was shining in his stall, and the golden bell was shining against the wall.

Constantes put the barley sugar in the manger to keep the horse quiet, and he began pushing the plugs into the holes of the bell, so that the bell should not give out its music. He put in forty plugs, but he dropped the last one among the straw, and he couldn't find it. So thought he, 'I'm off!' He took the bell under his arm, and got on the horse's back, and galloped away.

And the bell gave out a little tinkle from its unplugged hole.

The dragon sat up in bed and said, 'Was that my golden bell I heard tinkling?'

Said the dragoness, 'You're dreaming. It wasn't your golden bell. Go to sleep!'

So the dragon lay down.

But by and by he sat up again. 'I'm sure it was my golden bell tinkling!' he said. And he jumped out of bed and ran to the stable.

When he found that the silver horse was gone, and the golden bell was gone, he bellowed with rage. He looked out over the fields and vineyards and saw the silver horse shining in the dark, and he saw the black shape of a man on the horse's back.

'It's that Constantes again!' he bawled. And he bounded off after them.

There they were, Constantes galloping for his life, and the dragon pounding after him, all through the fields and the vineyards. The dragon in his rage was going even faster than the horse, and he was gaining.

'Villain!' bawled the dragon, 'Give me back my horse and bell! What new trick is this, you dog?'

And Constantes shouted over his shoulder, 'What I have done so far is nothing to what I will do!'

And he urged on the horse till it was going like the wind. He got through the gates of the city just as the dragon came up to them. So the dragon had to turn and go home.

Constantes gave the silver horse and the golden bell to the king. The king pulled the plugs out of the bell, and got on the horse, and rode round the city. The horse shone, and the bell rang very sweetly. The king was pleased; he gave Constantes three new suits of clothes. And Constantes was more in favour than before.

But the eldest brother went to the king and said, 'Constantes has got a swelled head. Do you know what he is saying now?'

Said the king, 'What is he saying?'

'He is saying that he can bring you the dragon himself.'

The king thought it would be grand to have a dragon to exhibit, so he sent for Constantes and said to him, 'Bring me the dragon.'

'I cannot do that,' said Constantes.

Said the king, 'Then why did you boast that you could? Take your choice: bring me the dragon, or lose your head.'

Constantes went out of the city into the vineyards. And there he met the old woman. Said he, 'You cannot help me this time, mother. I shall have to run away.'

Said the old woman, 'Why will you have to run away?'

And he told her.

Said the old woman, 'What rubbish! You needn't run away. Go to the king and ask him for a tattered suit, a hatchet, a saw, an awl,

15

a pound of nails, four ropes, and a false beard.' And she told him what else he must do.

So Constantes got those things from the king, and disguised himself as an old man, and went off to the mountain and began to hew down a plane tree near to the dragon's house.

The dragon saw him. He came out and said, 'What are you doing, old man?'

Said Constantes, 'I am to make a coffin for Constantes, who has just died.'

'Ah, the dog!' chuckled the dragon. 'Is he dead at last? And time he was! Here, let me help!' And he pulled up the tree as easily as pulling up a daisy.

Then they set to work together, making the coffin. When it was ready, Constantes said, 'I don't think it's big enough.'

'Not big enough!' said the dragon. 'Why, it's big enough for *me*!'

Said Constantes, 'No, it isn't.'

Said the dragon, 'Yes, it is.'

Said Constantes, 'Get in and try, then.'

And the dragon got in.

Then Constantes said, 'We'll just see if the lid fits.' He put on the lid and nailed it down, and tied the coffin round with two of the ropes.

'What are you doing, old fellow?' bawled the dragon. 'Let me out! The coffin fits!'

Said Constantes, 'So it does! Constantes has got you right and tight now!' He fetched his horse, which he had hidden behind a wall, and he made traces of the other two ropes, and he and the horse dragged the coffin along between them all the way to the city.

When he got to the palace, he said to the king, 'I have the dragon in a box in the courtyard.'

Said the eldest brother, 'Is the dragon wearing his ruby crown?'

'No, he is not,' said Constantes.

Said the eldest brother, 'Your majesty can't exhibit the dragon without his ruby crown.'

Said the king to Constantes, 'Go and fetch it.'

Constantes went out and met the old woman in the vineyard.

'Oh dear, oh dear, mother, my difficulties never end! Now I have to fetch the dragon's ruby crown!'

Said the old woman, 'That won't be easy. But if you keep your wits about you, you can manage it.' And she wrote a letter, as if from the dragon, and told Constantes to take it to the dragoness. This was the letter:

Dear Dragoness,

You are to put the bearer of this letter into the oven and roast him. When I come back I will have him for my supper. But first wrap my ruby crown in a duster and put it on your head, so that he shan't steal it before you roast him. For he's as cunning as a bag full of monkeys.

And Constantes went off with the letter to the dragon's house. And there was the dragoness looking out of the door.

'Good-day, dragoness.'

'Same to you, young man. What's your pleasure?'

'I've brought you a letter from the dragon,' said Constantes.

The dragoness took the letter. She was some time reading it, because she was slow-witted. Then she said, 'Well, sit you down, young man, whilst I make ready.'

The dragoness went away to heat up the oven. By and by she called Constantes into the kitchen. She had a big duster coiled round in a lump on the top of her head.

'Is that to keep your head clean?' said Constantes.

'Yes, it is,' said the dragoness. 'Because the ashes fly about so. Now, young man, my eyes aren't so good and the sun dazzles me.

Just you get on the shovel and cast a shadow, so's we may see if the fire's glowing. It's pies the dragon asked me to cook.'

'Oh, so it's pies, is it?' said Constantes. And he made as if to climb up on to the big shovel, and tumbled off again. He did this several times. Then he said, 'You'll have to show me how to do it, mistress dragon. I can't get the hang of it, somehow.'

Said the dragoness, 'Why, young man, where's your wits? You get on like this.'

She got up on to the shovel, and Constantes snatched the duster with the crown in it off her head, and gave her a push, and she slid off the shovel into the oven. And Constantes slammed the oven door, and ran off with the ruby crown.

'Now,' said he, when he got back to the courtyard. 'Here's the ruby crown, and it's time to open the coffin and exhibit the dragon.'

The king and all the courtiers seated themselves on the palace balcony, out of harm's way. Crowds of people looked out of every window.

'My eldest brother ought to have the honour of opening the coffin,' said Constantes. 'The exhibition was his idea.' So the king turned to the eldest brother, and said, 'Go and open the coffin.'

The eldest brother didn't want to, but what could he do? So he prised up the lid, and the dragon sprang out. Seeing no one near him but the man who had lifted the lid, he opened his great jaws, and swallowed the eldest brother at one gulp. Then, since nobody stopped him, he rushed out of the courtyard and galloped home.

He was shouting round the house for the dragoness, but he couldn't find her anywhere. Then he smelled something scorching, and he ran to the oven, and opened it. There was the dragoness, the scales melting off her with the heat. He pulled her out by the spike of her tail, and carried her off, and dived down into a lake with her.

And under the waters of that lake they have lived from that day; and have never more been seen by Constantes, or by anyone else.

2· *Chien Tang*

Once upon a time there was a mighty dragon called Chien Tang. Chien Tang lived in a well, and he served the Supreme Ruler of Heaven. It was Chien Tang's duty to fly up to the clouds and bring them down as rain upon the earth, that flowers might spring, and crops might grow. And it was his duty, also, when enough rain had fallen, to blow the clouds away with his mighty breath, and clear the sky. And, when he had done all this, it was his duty to return to his well and live there quietly until the earth needed watering again.

The people were grateful to Chien Tang; and very often they would gather round his well and sing his praises. And they dropped offerings into the well – flowers and poems written on silk, and little pictures. But one day there was a scoffer amongst the people, and he said, 'What a fuss to make about an old dragon!' And what did he do but crumple up some dirty rags, and make them into a ball, and drop them into the well.

Now in the midst of this ball of rags, the scoffer had put a paper with a message on it. And the message was, 'Pooh to you, Chien Tang!'

When Chien Tang unrolled the ball and read that message, he gave a tremendous roar. He rose up from his well, he flew up to the sky, he gathered the storm clouds in his fist, he beat their heads together till they thundered and lightninged, and poured down torrents of rain. The fields were drowned, the villages were washed

away, the people fled. And the torrents of rain poured down without cease for nine whole years.

Then the emperor, sorrowing for his people, sent up a prayer to the Supreme Ruler of Heaven. And the Supreme Ruler of Heaven laid hands on mighty Chien Tang and flung him down into the lake Tung Ting. And there he bound him to a pillar in the palace of the Dragon King of the lake, who was Chien Tang's brother.

Chien Tang was bound so tightly that he could only move the tip of his tail; and bound to that pillar he remained for two thousand years. And being tied up like that did not improve his temper.

Now Chien Tang's brother, the Dragon King of the lake, had a very beautiful daughter, and he gave her in marriage to a neighbouring dragon who was king of the river Ching. This river dragon was selfish and cruel; he treated his beautiful wife like a slave; and he set her to herd his flock of goats which he pastured on the banks of the river.

One day, a humble young student, whose name was Liu, was walking along the river bank, and he saw a beautiful girl herding goats. The girl looked very sorrowful; and though she was dressed like a peasant, and was doing a peasant's work, she did not *look* in the least like a peasant, for she had a royal air of dignity and grace. And, seeing her so sorrowful, Liu went up to her and bowed, and asked if there was any way in which he could serve her.

'Oh!' said she. 'If only you would take a letter to my father!'

She told him that she was the daughter of the Dragon King of lake Tung Ting. She told him also all about her own sad marriage.

'I would do anything for you,' said Liu. 'But, beautiful princess, how can I take a letter to your royal father, if he lives at the bottom of a lake?'

'If you will go to the lake,' said the dragon princess, 'you will see a tree growing on its margin, and the tree is taller than all the other trees around the lake. Take off your girdle, strike the tree three times with it, and you will be shown the way to my father's palace.'

And she gave Liu the letter which she had been carrying in her sleeve for a long time, hoping to find someone to deliver it.

Liu went to the lake, saw the tall tree, took off his girdle, and struck the tree three times with it. And at once the surface of the lake was stirred, and a young dragon came out of the water.

'Shut your eyes, friend Liu,' said the young dragon.

Liu shut his eyes, and immediately fell asleep.

When he woke up, he found himself in the throne room of a magnificent palace. And the splendour of that throne room, gleaming with pearls and rubies and amethyst and jade, was unequalled by anything that could be seen upon the surface of the earth. Courtiers and attendants, wearing robes of gold and silver scales, thronged the throne room; and they looked at Liu without speaking, yet not unkindly.

And then in walked the Dragon King himself. He had assumed the shape of a man, tall and dignified; but he wore a dragon crown of golden horns on his head. His flowing hair and beard were green, and he carried a jade tablet.

He, too, looked at Liu thoughtfully, but not unkindly. And after a while he said, 'How came you here? And how did you learn the secret of the tree?'

Liu bowed to the ground three times, for the Dragon King was godlike to behold. And then he answered, 'It was your honourable daughter who sent me with a letter to you. She told me the secret of the tree.'

And he gave the Dragon King the princess's letter.

The king read the letter, and began to weep. He showed the letter to the courtiers, and *they* began to weep. He sent for the princess's mother, and showed her the letter, and *she* began to weep. Now the throne room was filled with the sounds of weeping and wailing. The jewelled walls and the lofty ceiling caught the laments, and echoed them back:

'Alas! Alas! Alas for the poor princess! Alas for our dear daughter! Alas for baseness and cruelty! How shall we avenge this insult to our family?'

But suddenly the Dragon King held up his hand. 'Hush!' he called. 'Let us not mourn so loudly! It is right that we should weep; it is right that we should avenge this insult to our family. But we have forgotten my brother Chien. If once he hears what has happened, no pillar or chain will hold him!'

Then they hushed their voices. But it was too late. There came a roar as of a hundred thunderstorms: a red-scaled dragon, a thousand feet long, shot past them to the surface of the lake. Flames flashed from his eyes, his claws were spread wide, and on his back, and trailing behind him, was the mighty pillar to which he was still chained.

The fierce wind of that dragon's passing flung Liu to the ground; and almost before he could recover his senses and get to his feet again, the dragon came rushing back. He was carrying the princess in his arms, and he was no longer dragging his pillar. The first thing he had done was to swallow the river dragon. The second thing he had done was to shoot up to heaven, and beg forgiveness of the Supreme Ruler, who had mercifully released him from his pillar. And the third thing he had done was to bring the smiling princess back to her parents.

Now all their sadness was turned to gladness. The jewelled walls and the high roof of the throne room re-echoed with laughter and cries of joy. A mighty feast was prepared, and the grateful Dragon King of lake Tung Ting offered Liu his daughter's hand in marriage: an offer which Liu as gratefully accepted.

So it came about that the humble young student, Liu, married a princess. And his life was indeed a marvellous one. He was granted the power of being equally at home under the water or on land. And he was also granted a dragon's life, which lasts for ten thousand years.

3· Stan Bolovan

Once upon a time there was a man called Stan Bolovan. He had a little house, and he had a little orchard, and he had a good little cow, and he had a good little wife. And if the wife comes last, it is not because she was least; but because, whilst his little house and his little orchard and his little cow made Stan feel happy, his wife made him feel unhappy. Because she was always crying.

She cried after breakfast, she cried after dinner, she cried after supper, she cried when she went to bed. And she wouldn't tell Stan what she was crying about – that was the worst of it.

'Don't *bother*!' she said. 'Leave me alone! You wouldn't understand.'

But Stan did bother. He bothered after breakfast, he bothered after dinner, he bothered after supper, he bothered when he went to bed. Until at last she did tell him. And what do you think? She was crying because they had no children.

Stan hadn't thought anything about it before; but now he did think about it, and it seemed to him a great pity. It made him very sad, and *he* felt like crying. There they were now, the two of them, both miserable.

So one day Stan took a journey to consult a magician. The magician was sitting on the steps outside his door. He was wearing a robe patterned with suns and moons and stars. He had a big crystal globe on his knees, and he was looking down into this crystal globe and twiddling his thumbs, whilst Stan told of the sorrow of himself and his wife.

When Stan had told all, the magician stopped twiddling his thumbs, and drew his forefinger across the crystal globe, as if he were tracing a picture in it.

Said he, 'Are you sure what you are asking for? Children can be a great burden.'

'But sorrow is a greater burden,' said Stan. 'A joyful burden is but a light one. Only give us children!' And he fell on his knees at the magician's feet, and kept crying out, 'Give us children, my lord! Give us children!'

'Oh, all right,' said the magician. 'Have it your own way.' And he took his crystal globe under his arm, and went into his house, and shut the door.

Stan was tired, and Stan was hot, and Stan was dusty before he got home that evening. But, all the same, the sorrow was lifted from his heart. And when he drew near his little house, he heard a clear ringing laugh. And that was his wife's laugh, that he hadn't heard for long enough. He heard other sounds, too: a chattering and a chirruping, and a clapping of hands, and a patter of feet. And when he turned the corner of the lane, and came in view of his little house, and his little garden, and his little orchard – what did he see?

What did he not see? Children in the orchard, children in the garden, children tumbling out through the door, children crowding at every window! And all of them the same size, and all of them very little, and very fat, and very impudent-looking, and all of them laughing and shouting, and not one of them with a stitch of clothing to bless itself with. And in the midst of this crowd of little children stood his wife, laughing as merrily as any of them.

'Heavens alive!' exclaimed Stan. 'How many of them are there? A hundred at least!'

'But not one too many!' laughed his wife.

Well, maybe not. But a hundred children need some feeding and some clothing. Very soon the children had eaten up all there was to eat, and Stan's wife had cut up all her petticoats and chemises to make little garments for them, and still they were half of them naked. And though Stan was happy, and his wife was happy, yet when he heard the children crying out, 'Daddy, I'm hungry! Daddy, I'm hungry!' – well, it was time to think a bit.

So Stan scratched his head and thought and thought. And then he said, 'Old woman, this won't do. I'll have to go out into the world and find something to eat.' He was very hungry himself, if the truth be known, for all the cow's milk had been given to the children; and the children had eaten all the little green apples off the trees in the orchard, and his wife had made up every scrap of flour into little cakes for them, and Stan hadn't eaten a morsel himself since goodness knows when.

So off he went, and the way seemed very long, because he didn't know exactly where he was going. And towards evening he came to a great sheepfold, and a shepherd was driving the ewes and lambs into the fold for the night.

'If I wait till dark,' thought Stan, 'I might be able to pick up a lamb or two, and carry them home. I know it's not exactly right; but then, with a hundred hungry children – what can a man do?'

So he hid himself, and waited till night.

There was a moon, but there were also clouds, and Stan was waiting till the clouds should come up over the moon, when he heard a rushing sound, and down through the air swooped a dragon. The dragon scooped up four lambs, one in each of his feet, and took two ewes in his jaws and flew off again.

Now there was pandemonium in the sheepfold – lambs bleating, sheep baaing, and the poor frightened creatures jumping over the hurdles and running in all directions. The shepherd was shouting and running, his dog was barking and rounding up the sheep, and Stan was puffing and panting (for he was rather fat) and doing what he could to help. When the sheep were back in the fold, Stan and the shepherd sat down side by side, and the shepherd began to beat the ground with his fists and wail.

'Every night it's the same!' he wailed. 'Every night that dragon comes to rob me, and soon I shan't have a sheep left!'

Stan had been helping himself to some of the shepherd's bread and cheese, and taking swigs from the shepherd's water bottle: now with food inside him he was feeling equal to anything, and a very bold thought came to him.

'What will you give me if I rid you of that dragon?' he said.

'Three fine fat rams, and one of every three sheep, and one of every three lambs,' said the shepherd.

'*And* a bit of food for myself to keep me going till the dragon comes again?'

'As much food as you can eat,' said the shepherd.

'Well then, that's a bargain,' said Stan.

Stan hadn't a notion of how he was going to get rid of the dragon. But he was so grateful to have plenty to eat that he spent the next day happily enough with the shepherd. It was only when night came, and the moon rose up clear and full in a cloudless sky, that he began to feel a quaking of terror in his stomach. By and by the quakings became so unbearable that he was all but running off into the night and making for home. It was only the picture of those hundred children, all clamouring for food, that kept him waiting for the dragon.

At midnight came the rushing sound, and down through the air swooped the dragon, with the moon shining on his scaly back, and lighting up the horns on his head and the cruel spikes on his wings.

'Now or never!' thought Stan. And he stood up boldly at the gate of the sheepfold, and shouted, '*Stop!*'

28

The dragon clattered to the ground, and stood there staring.

'Well I never!' said he. 'And who may *you* be?'

And Stan answered, 'I am Stan Bolovan. The Great Stan Bolovan, who eats rocks all night, and in the daytime gobbles up the flowers on the mountains. And if you touch those sheep, I will gobble up *you!*'

'You'll have to fight me first,' said the dragon. But his voice trembled a little; because, for all his vicious look, he was a coward at heart.

'Fight *you!*' bellowed Stan. 'What next? Don't you know that I can kill you with one breath? Aye, and carry your corpse up into the mountains, and make you into a sandwich with my flowers!'

The dragon was really frightened now. 'Well, good night!' he said hastily.

'Hey! Hey! Not so fast!' said Stan. 'You and I have an account to settle.'

'What for?'

'For the sheep you've stolen. They all belong to me. That fellow you see skulking behind a bush yonder is only one of my hired shepherds. So pay up, or it will be the worse for you!'

The dragon hadn't any money. He was turning yellow with fright. He thought the great Stan Bolovan was going to make him into mincemeat and put him in a sandwich to eat with his flowers. 'Tell you what,' he said. 'You come along home with me. My old mother has bags of money. If you'll stay with us for three days, and keep her in a good temper by helping her with this and that, I can promise you she'll give you seven sacks full of ducats a day.'

To live for three days with two dragons! Stan didn't fancy it. But when he thought of twenty-one sacks full of ducats, and of the food it would buy for his hungry children, he said, 'All right, I'll come.'

So off they went, Stan and the dragon, to the dragon's house. And when they got near it, Stan could see the old mother dragon looking out, and her great eyes were shining like two lamps, and lighting up the path, and the trees, yes, and the very grass blades.

'*What!*' she called out. 'No sheep!'

And she flew into a rage, and flames and sparks came out of her nostrils.

'My mother's a bit of a tartar,' whispered the dragon to Stan. 'You'd best stay where you are, and I'll go in and explain things to her.'

Stan was glad enough to stay where he was. The dragon and his mother went into the house. Again Stan thought he would run away; and again he thought of his hungry children, and waited.

Inside the house, the dragon was whispering to his mother. 'I've brought home a most terrible fellow! He eats rocks, and makes dragons into sandwiches. We must get rid of him somehow!'

The mother dragon gave a yelp of laughter that shook the house. 'You just leave him to me! I'll fix him!'

So the dragon called Stan in.

Stan didn't sleep well that night, though they gave him a tremendous bed with a feather mattress that billowed up all round him like the waves of the sea. But he kept dreaming that the mother dragon was setting the bed on fire with the lamps of her eyes.

In the morning, she said to him, 'I would like to see which is the stronger, you or my son.' And she took down an enormous club bound round with seven hoops of iron. 'Now, try which one of you can throw this the farthest.'

The dragon took the club and went to the door. He twirled the club lightly three times round his head. He gave it a fling. And it fell to the ground three miles away.

He and Stan walked after it. There it lay, half buried in the ground. Stan knew that even if he had seven strong men to help him, he could never so much as lift that club. So he stood looking down at it, and sighing.

'What a pity!' he said.

'*What's* a pity?' said the dragon.

'It's such a beautiful club,' said Stan. 'I was thinking it's a terrible pity it should cause your death.'

'What d'you mean – my *death*?' cried the dragon.

'It's this way,' said Stan. 'Whatever I throw always comes back to me, because my hands are like magnets. It wouldn't hurt *me*, of course, I'm too strong. But it might hit you on the head in passing. And then it would crack your skull.'

'Oh well, you needn't be in a hurry to throw, after all,' said the dragon. 'Let's have something to eat first.'

'I'll wait all day, if you like,' said Stan. '*I'm* not in a hurry to crack your skull.'

So the dragon went home and fetched a pile of food, and they sat by the club and feasted till night came. And then Stan stood up and stared at the sky.

Said the dragon, 'What are you looking at?'

'At the moon,' said Stan. 'I'm waiting for it to go down the sky. Don't you see it's exactly in my way? But, of course, if you're in a hurry, I'll throw the club up now. Mind you, it will land slap in the moon, and I expect it will stick there. You don't mind losing it, I suppose?'

The dragon did mind losing his club. It had been left to him by his grandfather, and he prized it.

'*Don't* throw it!' he said.

'Oh but I must!' said Stan. 'Your mother said so. It was to be a trial of strength.'

'Let me throw it for you,' said the dragon. 'She'll never know.'

But Stan said no, and kept on saying no, till at last the dragon offered him seven sacks full of ducats not to throw the club into the moon. And Stan said, 'Oh, very well.' And the dragon picked up the club and threw it back towards the house, and it landed a mile behind the house.

'Three miles to you, and four miles to me,' said Stan. 'I've won!'

'Yes, you've won,' said the dragon gloomily.

And he went galloping into the house, and told his mother that he had had all the difficulty in the world to prevent Stan from throwing the club into the moon.

Oh dear! The mother dragon began to feel a bit frightened, too!

Next morning she said, 'Now you two go and fetch me some water.' And she gave them twelve buffalo skins and told them to go on filling them till night. They went to the spring, and the dragon filled the twelve skins, carried them home, and brought them back empty.

'Now it's your turn,' said he to Stan.

Stan took a knife from his pocket, and began to scratch up the earth round the spring.

Said the dragon, 'What are you doing?'

'Digging up the spring,' said Stan. 'It's a waste of time carrying water in little skin fulls. Might as well carry the whole lot at once.'

'No, no, you mustn't do that!' cried the dragon. 'My grand-daddy made that spring. Leave it alone! Here, *I'll* carry your skins for you!'

'No,' said Stan; and went on with his digging.

So, in the end, the dragon offered Stan another seven sacks full of ducats not to dig up the spring. And Stan said, 'Oh, all right.'

The dragon carried the skins full of water all day, and in the evening he was tired and cross. But Stan lay and snored on his feather bed: he had only to stay with the dragons for another twenty-four hours, and he felt he was getting the better of them.

The next morning, the old mother dragon told them to go to the forest and fetch her some wood. So they went to the forest; and the dragon began pulling up the trees as if they were small sticks, and laying them neatly in rows. But Stan climbed to the top of a tree that had a wild vine trailed about it. And he tied the top of the tree to the top of the next tree with the vine.

Said the dragon, 'What *are* you doing up there?'

'Tying the trees together,' said Stan. 'Saves time. Then I can take the whole forest back at one go.'

'No, no!' cried the dragon. 'My grand-daddy planted this forest! Leave it alone!'

'I won't,' said Stan. '*I'm* not going to run backwards and forwards with two or three trees at a time.'

Then the dragon offered Stan seven times seven sacks full of ducats to leave the forest alone. And Stan said, 'All right.' And the dragon ran backwards and forwards all day carrying the firewood home; and Stan spent a lazy day watching him.

So the third day came to an end, and in the morning Stan would be free to go home, with three sacks full of ducats for each day, and seven more sacks full of ducats for not throwing the club into the moon, and seven more for not digging up the spring, and seven times seven more for not pulling up the forest. And the only thing that troubled him was how to get those ducats home.

But that night, when Stan had gone to bed, the dragon and his mother sat in the parlour and had a long talk. And Stan put his ear to the floorboards, and listened.

'We shall be ruined!' wailed the dragon.

'No, we shan't,' said the old mother.

'What can we do?' wailed the dragon.

'You must kill him this very night,' said the old mother.

'I dursn't!' wailed the dragon. 'He's too strong, he'll kill *me!*'

'No, he won't,' said the old mother. 'You wait till he's asleep. And then take your grand-daddy's club and hit him on the head.'

'Ho, ho! will you?' thought Stan.

33

The dragon and his mother blew out the candles and went to bed. 'Wait till you hear him snoring,' whispered the old mother.

But Stan got up and fetched the pigs' trough, filled it with earth, laid it on his bed, and covered it up with the blankets. Then he got under the bed and began to snore loudly.

The dragon came tiptoeing in with the club. He brought the club down with a tremendous whack on the top of the pigs' trough. And from under the bed Stan gave a tremendous groan. The dragon went tiptoeing out again; and when Stan heard his snores shaking the house, he got up, carried the pigs' trough down into the yard, and made everything tidy.

In the morning, when Stan came down to breakfast, the dragon and his mother gaped as if they were seeing a ghost.

'How – how did – did you sleep?' stammered the dragon.

'Not too badly,' said Stan. 'A rat ran over my face and tickled me with his tail. But I caught him, and sent him about his business. I don't think he'll trouble me tonight.'

'*Tonight!*' gasped the dragon. 'I thought you were going home this morning!'

'No,' said Stan. 'I find myself pretty comfortable here. So I've decided to stay on for a bit.'

The dragon and his mother went into another room and began to quarrel.

'It's all your fault – why did you ever bring him here?' said the mother dragon.

'As if I could help it!' said her son. 'He was going to make me into a sandwich!'

'You've ruined me!' said his mother. 'I'll have to give him all the gold I've got.'

'Better be ruined than let him stay another hour!' said the son.

So the mother dragon fetched all the sacks she could lay hands on, and began cramming them full of ducats. 'We're but simple folk,' she said to Stan. 'And though we've enjoyed your company, we're not used to visitors. In fact, my son and I are thinking of going to the seaside for a change. So here's a little present for you.'

Stan stood and stared at the sacks full of ducats. There were eighty-three of them, all bursting full of gold pieces.

'What are you waiting for?' said the dragon.

'I'm just thinking,' said Stan. 'What will my people say when I arrive home with that miserable little lot? They'll say, "The great Stan Bolovan has been away only three days, and he's come home as weak as a dragon." No – I couldn't do it. I'll have to stay.'

The dragon gave a shriek, and his mother gave a shriek. They said Stan should have seven times as many sacks, or even seven times seven as many, if only he would go home.

'Well, well,' said Stan, 'I see you don't want me to stay, and I'm not the kind of fellow to make myself disagreeable. So I'll go – but only on one condition.'

'*Any* condition. What *is* the condition?' shrieked the dragon.

'That you carry the sacks home for me yourself,' said Stan. 'Then I shan't be put to shame before my friends.'

In an instant, the dragon was seizing up the sacks in his claws and piling them on his back.

'Well, good-bye,' said Stan to the mother dragon. 'And thank you for your hospitality.'

'Don't mention it,' said she; and slammed the door in his face, and locked it.

So Stan and the dragon walked off towards Stan's home. And when they got near, Stan could hear his children shouting.

Said he to the dragon, 'My dear friend, I am feeling rather worried about you. I have a hundred children, and they are all as strong as I am. They don't mean any harm, of course; but they are rather rough. And in their playfulness they just *might* tear you to pieces.'

36

Torn to pieces by a hundred little Stan Bolovans! The dragon trembled so much that he let all the sacks tumble to the ground. And then the children, who had heard Stan's voice, and who were, moreover, exceedingly hungry, having had nothing to eat since Stan went away, came rushing out, waving their knives and forks and shouting, 'Give us dragon's flesh! We will have dragon's flesh!'

'I told you . . .' began Stan.

But the dragon didn't wait to be told anything. He gave a loud scream and rushed away, vowing to himself that he would never come near Stan's house again.

So Stan and his wife and his hundred children gathered up the gold, and had plenty to eat, and plenty to wear, and plenty to spend for the rest of their lives.

4 · *My Lord Bag of Rice*

A man called Hidesato was returning home from a journey. His road led him past a mountain, and under the mountain was a lake with a bridge spanning it. That way, over the lake, was the way Hidesato wished to go; but, right across the road in front of the bridge, lay an enormous dragon.

Hidesato was a very brave man. So, instead of running away, he clambered right over the dragon, and went calmly on his way across the bridge. He hadn't gone many steps when he heard a voice calling him. He turned round, and saw a majestic-looking man beckoning to him. The man had red-gold hair, and was wearing a dragon-crown.

'Hullo!' said Hidesato. 'Did you call me?'

The majestic-looking man came up to him and said, 'Yes, Hidesato, I called you. I am the Dragon King of this lake, and for many days now I have been lying across the road in my dragon shape, waiting for a man who showed no fear. Up on the mountain lives a monstrous centipede; and every evening he comes down and enters my palace and destroys my children and my grandchildren. Only a brave mortal can destroy him, and so I have watched and waited.'

'I will do my best,' said Hidesato. 'I am not often afraid. As you see, I am carrying my bow and arrows, and I am a good shot. But whether I can destroy a monster or not, I do not know.'

The Dragon King took Hidesato down to his palace in the

middle of the lake to wait till evening. There they feasted on lotus leaves and flowers. And whilst they feasted, ten little goldfish entertained them with elegant dancing, and ten carps made sweet music on instruments shaped like shells. Hidesato was enjoying himself very much, when suddenly there came a most tremendous crashing and booming, as if the whole universe had turned into one great thunderstorm.

Hidesato and the Dragon King ran on to the balcony, and looked towards the mountain. And the mountain was hidden from top to bottom by the great brown coils of an enormous centipede. The centipede's eyes were two huge balls of fire, and its hundred feet, as it crawled down the mountain, were like a moving chain of lighted lanterns.

Hidesato fitted an arrow to his bow, and shot. The arrow struck the centipede clean in the middle of its flat forehead. But the arrow glanced off harmlessly; the centipede merely flickered out a fiery tongue, as much as to say, 'Pooh!' and still it came crawling on.

Hidesato fitted a second arrow to his bow, and shot again. Again the arrow hit the centipede clean in the middle of its forehead, and again glanced harmlessly aside; and again the centipede flickered out its fiery tongue, and came crawling, crawling on.

Now Hidesato had only one arrow left. What could he do?

'Spit on it!' cried the Dragon King. 'The spit of a brave man has power in it!'

Hidesato spat on the tip of his arrow, and fitted the arrow to his bow, and shot. And the arrow struck the centipede full in the middle of its flat forehead. But this time the arrow did not glance aside; it went clean through the centipede's head.

The centipede stopped moving. The two huge balls of fire that were its eyes dwindled and dimmed. The lighted chain of lanterns that were its hundred feet flickered, and wavered, and went out. Now all that could be seen were the two little balls of fire, growing smaller and smaller and smaller, until they, too, were swallowed up in darkness.

Hidesato stood beside the Dragon King on the balcony. He could hear nothing but the Dragon King's sigh of thankfulness, and he could see nothing at all. An awful blackness and an awful silence lay over the mountain and the lake. And then, suddenly, the blackness was torn by streak after streak of forked lightning. Peal after peal of thunder clattered about Hidesato's ears; the mountain flashed into sight at one moment and disappeared the next; and the Dragon King's palace shuddered and swayed like a reed in a gale.

And then it seemed to Hidesato that the whole world was falling away beneath him; he, too, shuddered and swayed, and sank down at the Dragon King's feet.

When he came to himself it was morning. The sun was shining brilliantly, the sky was blue, the top of the mountain was glittering white, and in the sparkling blue waters of the lake lay the dead body of the centipede. The ten little goldfish were dancing their elegant dances, the ten carps were playing on their shell instruments, the table was spread, and again the Dragon King and Hidesato feasted on lotus leaves and flowers.

When they had feasted, Hidesato stood up and said it was time for him to go.

'I will bring you to the end of the bridge,' said the Dragon King. He and Hidesato walked together; and behind them walked a retinue of fishes turned into men, and bearing five gifts. At the end of the bridge, the Dragon King bowed to Hidesato, and went back to his palace; but the retinue of fishes-turned-men marched on as far as Hidesato's house. And there they laid down their five gifts before the house, and vanished.

The gifts were these: two bells, a bag of rice, a roll of silk, and a cooking pot. Such gifts may not sound a very great reward for slaying a monster, but they were great gifts, never the less. The bag of rice was no sooner emptied than it filled itself again; you might unroll and unroll that bale of silk, and still there was no end to it; and the cooking pot cooked everything that was put into it without the need of fire.

Only the bells contained no magic but their own sweet music, and Hidesato presented them to the temple. From his rice bag and his cooking pot he provided himself with food; with the silk he traded. From a simple, poor man, he became immensely rich; and though he had no wish to change his name, it was changed for him. No one called him Hidesato any more. Everyone called him *My Lord Bag of Rice*.

5 · The Nine Doves

Once upon a time there was a princess who lived in a glass tower, because the king, her father, wished to keep her safe. She had beautiful dresses to wear, and servants to wait on her, and the most delicious food to eat; but her food had always to be served up to her without bones, because the king was afraid she might choke herself. And the glass of her tower was frosted glass, because the king was afraid she might see something ugly in the world outside and be frightened. But then, she couldn't see anything pretty in the world outside, either; so it was not much of a life she lived, poor girl.

One day, as she was eating her dinner, she said to her serving maid, 'Is all meat the same as the meat I eat?'

'No, your royal highness,' said the maid. 'Our meat has bone in it.'

The princess put down her knife and fork and pushed her plate aside. 'I will not eat what no one else eats,' she said. 'Bring me some meat like the meat you eat.'

So the serving maid ran down to tell the cook, and the cook sent up a nicely grilled chop.

The princess cut the meat off the bone and ate it. Then she looked at what was left on her plate, and said, 'So this is what you call a bone?'

'Yes, your royal highness,' said the maid.

The princess picked up the bone and tried to bite it. And since she could not bite it, she threw the bone at the glass of the tower,

43

and broke a little window in it. 'Oh, what fun!' she said, peeping through the window. 'Now I can see the world!'

That afternoon, as the princess sat alone, she saw nine doves flying past the little window. Eight of the doves were black, and one was white. The black doves flew straight on; but the white dove, when it saw the princess, circled round once or twice, and then flew in through the window.

'Oh, you pretty thing!' cried the princess. 'Do let me catch you!'

The dove fluttered about the room, and the princess ran about after it; but she could never quite get her hands on it. Then the dove fluttered to the floor, and the princess stooped, and a ring slipped off her finger. And what did that dove do, but pick up the ring in its beak, and fly off with it out through the window.

The next afternoon, the nine doves, eight of them black, and one of them white, flew past the window again. And again the black doves flew straight on; and again the white dove circled round once or twice, and then flew in through the window.

'I'll catch you today, pretty bird!' cried the princess.

But the white dove fluttered here and fluttered there, always just out of the princess's reach. And then it fluttered to the floor, and the princess made a jump to catch it, and a bracelet slipped from her wrist. And the white dove picked up the bracelet in its beak, and flew off with it, out through the window.

'If it comes again, I *will* catch it!' said the princess.

And the next day, the nine doves, the eight black and the one white, flew past the window yet again. And the white dove flew in through the window and fluttered round the room, and the princess flapped at it with her handkerchief, thinking to drive it into a corner. But the dove caught the handkerchief in its beak, and the princess was so surprised that she let go. And the dove flew away through the window with the handkerchief.

That evening, the king came to pay his daughter a visit. He saw the broken glass, and was worried.

Said he, 'How did this happen?'

Said the princess, 'Oh, it just broke' – for she did not want to get her maid into trouble about the bone.

Said the king, 'It must be repaired. But it is very special glass. It came from the east; it may take months to get another piece. And I can't let you stay here until it *is* mended. Why – *anything* might come in!'

So he sent the princess to stay with her godmother in the country. The godmother was lazy; she couldn't be bothered to look after the princess as strictly as the king had done. But she told the princess she had better not go out of the garden. The garden was a pretty one; the princess spent most of her time in it; she liked it much better than the glass tower. And whenever she saw any people passing along the road, she would run to the gate, and ask them if they had seen her ring, or her bracelet, or her hand-kerchief.

But nobody had.

Near the godmother's house was a cottage, where a simpleton lived with his widowed mother. Said the simpleton one day, 'Mother dear, they say a beautiful princess stands at the gate of yonder house and talks to passers by. *I* am going to talk to the princess.'

'You will do nothing of the sort!' said his mother.

'Oh yes, I will,' said the simpleton.

His mother tried to dissuade him, but the simpleton was stubborn. So at last she said, 'Well then, go to the forest and get me some wood, that I may make a fire and wash your shirt. If you must go and chatter to the princess, you shall at least go clean!'

The simpleton took his little axe and his little donkey, and went to the forest. He tied the donkey to a tree stump, and said, 'Now my darling little donkey, you must wait patiently whilst I go and get the wood. But I would like the time to pass pleasantly for you, so here is a carrot. Munch away at that, my little donkey, and be good.'

The little donkey took the carrot, and the simpleton took his little axe, and went on a bit farther into the forest, where he knew there was a fallen tree that would be easy to chop. And he had only chopped up a few faggots, when what did he see but his little donkey trotting merrily past him.

'Whey-hey! Whey-ho! you bad little donkey!' he shouted. 'Didn't I tell you to wait patiently?'

And he ran after the little donkey to catch it.

The little donkey trotted merrily on, till it came to a great tree with a black door in it. And at that door the little donkey stood still. The simpleton had just stretched out his hand to catch hold of the bridle, when the door swung open, and the little donkey went through it, and the simpleton went after the little donkey.

'I'm seeing things today!' said the simpleton.

What he saw was a staircase going up and up; and the little donkey was going up the staircase. So the simpleton went up after it. By and by they came to a great room, and the little donkey went in, and the simpleton followed. And he was just going to lay hold of the little donkey, when that little donkey disappeared.

So there was the simpleton all alone in the great room; and he couldn't see any way out of it. Because the door had disappeared also.

At one end of the room was a fire with a cauldron hanging over it. The cauldron was bubbling and steaming, and the steam had a savoury smell. The simpleton lifted the lid and peered into the cauldron. What did he see? He saw two partridges cooked ready for eating.

'Oh ho!' said he, 'I'm not meant to starve here!'

And he took one partridge out of the cauldron, and slipped into a cupboard beside the fire to eat it.

'Safer the bite if out of sight!' he said.

He had eaten all the meat and was sucking the bones, when he heard a soft *flit-flit flutter*, like dozens of little wings beating against something hard. He peeped through a chink in the cupboard and saw nine doves, eight of them black and one of them white, come flying through the wall of the room. The doves settled on the floor and shook their feathers, and the white one turned into a handsome young man. But the eight black ones turned into eight black dragons.

'Oh my goodness!' thought the simpleton. 'I don't know that I much like what I'm seeing today. One dragon is bad enough! But *eight* – oh, my goodness! What next, I wonder?'

What next was that the dragons went back through the wall, and the handsome young man clapped his hands. Then in came a maid with a basin and towel, and the handsome young man washed his hands. The maid took the basin and towel away through the wall, and came back wheeling a table laid for dinner. Then she went to the cauldron and lifted the lid.

'Master,' she said, 'I put two partridges in to cook, and now there is only one!'

The simpleton began to tremble. 'What shall I do?' he thought. 'If she looks in the cupboard, I shall slap her!'

But the maid didn't look in the cupboard, she just stood staring into the cauldron, and the handsome young man said, 'Never mind, serve it up. It doesn't matter!'

And he ate as if it didn't matter, either, pushing the food about, and sighing between each mouthful. And the simpleton thought, 'What a waste! I might as well have eaten both birds for all *he* cares!'

The handsome young man clapped his hands again, and the maid cleared the dishes off the table, and went out with them through the wall. So there was the handsome young man left alone, sitting at the table.

And what did he do, but take a little lace handkerchief out of his pocket and kiss it, and spread it out on the table. Then he took a bracelet out of his pocket and kissed it, and laid it on the handkerchief. And then he took a ring out of his pocket, and kissed that, and laid it beside the bracelet.

Then he began to weep.

'Oh my princess, my princess!' he wept. 'What has become of you? I fly past your tower. I fly through the window. I fly and I seek you, but I cannot find you!'

And he laid his head down on the table and sobbed.

He was still sobbing when there came a sound like the beating of flails on iron. He had only just time to jump up and thrust ring, bracelet and handkerchief into his pocket, when the eight black dragons came flying back through the wall. They landed on the floor, blowing fire out of their nostrils; they rattled their wings and turned into eight black doves. The young man waved his fingers and turned into a white dove. Then they all flew away through the wall. And the simpleton came out of the cupboard.

'I'm not liking this at all!' said he. 'What next, I wonder?'

What next was that a door opened in the wall, and his little donkey was standing in the doorway. 'Oh, my darling little donkey!' cried the simpleton, and he ran over to it. The little donkey turned and went down the staircase, and the simpleton went after it. When they got to the bottom, the black door in the tree was shut against them. But the little donkey pushed with its nose, and the door opened, and they went through. And there they were, standing in the forest again.

They went to the place where the faggots were lying, and the simpleton took his little axe and chopped up a few more. Then he looked up, and he couldn't see his little donkey anywhere. So he put the faggots in a sack, and started to walk home. And when he came to the tree stump, there was his little donkey tied up to it, and lipping the ground for an end of carrot he had let fall.

The simpleton flung his arms round the little donkey's neck, and kissed its nose. 'Oh my darling, clever little donkey!' he cried. 'I tied you up, and you got loose by yourself, and tied yourself up again – all to save me trouble!'

He got on his little donkey's back, and rode home. He had a fine tale to tell his mother, but she didn't believe a word of it. She lit a fire and got the water hot, and washed and dried his shirt. The simpleton washed his face: he didn't want to, but his mother made him. And then, with a clean face, and wearing his clean shirt, he ran off to talk to the princess.

The princess was standing at the garden gate, and she asked the simpleton, as she asked everyone, if he had seen a ring, and a bracelet, and a handkerchief.

'Oh yes, I've seen them,' said the simpleton.

'When? Where?' cried the princess.

So then the simpleton told the princess all the strange things that had happened. And the princess believed him, though his mother hadn't. 'Take me there!' said the princess.

'No, I won't take you,' said the simpleton.

'Why not?' said the princess.

The simpleton didn't know why not. He just didn't want to take her. He wasn't used to walking about with princesses. Now that he had seen her, he wanted to go home. But the princess begged him very prettily. She picked a flower and put it in his buttonhole, and told him what a fine fellow he was. She flattered him till he was all one big grin, and he said, 'Oh, all right, come on then.'

He took her to the black door in the tree, and the door opened for them, and they went up the staircase into the big room. The

49

simpleton and the princess hid in the cupboard, and everything happened as it had happened before: except that when the handsome young man sat sobbing with his head on the table, the princess came out of the cupboard and ran to him, and said, 'Don't cry any more. I'm here!'

Well, it wasn't many minutes after that before they were telling each other all about themselves. The handsome young man told the princess that he had loved her from the first moment he had seen her, when he flew into her glass tower in the shape of a dove. He told her, also, that he was a prince, whom the eight dragons had stolen out of his cradle. He told her that they had tried to turn him into a dragon, because they wanted a son; but they could not turn him into a dragon, try as they would. All they could do was to change him into a dove. So, whilst they went in their dragon shapes, he was still a prince; but when they changed into the shape of black doves, he changed into a dove also—a white one.

'And how can I ask the hand of a princess, even though I love her with my whole soul,' he said, 'when half my time I am a dove, and only half my time a prince?'

The princess smiled. 'A dove can be loved also,' she said. 'But come – now whilst you are still a prince, and before the dragons return, let us escape from this place!'

So they took each other by the hand and ran through the wall, which melted like mist before them; and the simpleton jumped out of the cupboard and ran after them. He ran home stammering out to his mother a tale she didn't believe. But the princess and the prince ran on till they came to the glass tower. And they ran into that tower; and, for the time, they were safe.

But by and by the eight black dragons came back into the room inside the tree, and alighted on the floor and changed themselves into black doves. The princess was sitting in a little low chair in her room at the top of the tower; and the prince was sitting at her

feet with his head on her knee. He was telling her all over again how much he loved her, when suddenly he was silent. The princess looked down, and there on her knee was a little white dove, looking up into her face with tears in its eyes.

'Oh my darling, my darling!' said the princess. '*Don't* cry! I'm here with you still!' And she took the dove in her hands and ran with it to the king, and told him the whole story, and said that the dove, and no one else, must be her husband.

'But this is a very astonishing and awkward thing,' said the king, 'that you should want to marry a dove!'

'He isn't always a dove,' she said. 'You will see by and by.'

Meanwhile, the eight black doves were flying round and round the tower. But the glass had been mended, and they couldn't get in. So they turned into dragons again, and flew away. And the white dove turned into a handsome prince.

When the king saw the prince, he said, 'Um, yes, I see there is some sense in what you say, my daughter. But it is all very awkward. However, the two of you had better get married at once, whilst the bridegroom is still presentable.'

So they were married.

But it is a wearisome thing to be cooped up for ever in a glass tower, and one day the prince said, 'Let us go out and walk in the garden, even if it is only for half an hour.'

And they went out to walk in the garden. But they hadn't been walking for ten minutes, when the eight black doves flew by, and the prince turned into a white dove and flew after them.

The princess ran to her father. 'Build me a house,' she said, 'and let it be surrounded on all sides by a high iron wall, and let there be only one gate in the wall, and let that gate be of solid iron also.'

The king built the house for her, and the princess took a little serving maid with her, and went to live there.

And the princess sent her serving maid to the simpleton with a letter, and a message bidding him take the letter to the room inside the tree, and deliver it to the prince.

Said the simpleton, 'I won't go there!'

But the serving maid gave him a kiss, and he grinned and said, 'Give me two more kisses, and I'll go.'

The serving maid gave him two more kisses, and the simpleton went with the letter to the door in the tree, and up the long staircase, and into the room. He hid in the cupboard and waited for the doves to come. And when the white dove had changed into a prince, and the black doves had changed into dragons, and the prince was alone, the simpleton came out of the cupboard and gave the prince the letter. The prince kissed the letter and read it, and said to the simpleton, 'Tell the princess I will do what she says.'

And the simpleton went back to the princess and told her, 'He will do what you said.' And the princess waited and watched.

Then, one day, the nine doves came flying round the little house with the iron fence, and the white dove flew in front of the others. And when he flew up to the iron gate, the princess and her maid opened the gate, and the white dove flew in. And immediately the princess and her maid clanged the gate shut. And the eight black doves flew at the gate, beating with their wings, but they could not get in, for the gate was made of one piece of solid iron. So the eight black doves turned into eight black dragons, and battered and bit and clawed at the gate; but the gate stood firm. They could not open it, nor break it down, and in their rage they burst. And that was the end of them.

The princess looked round smiling to greet her prince. But what did she see? No prince, but a white dove fallen on the bed and struggling and gasping for breath. For the eight dragons, before they flew out as eight black doves, had stuck three pins through the feathers on the white dove's head, and until these pins were pulled out it could not change back into a man.

The dove was panting, its wings were fluttering very feebly. Its eyes were shut, and it seemed to be dying. The princess took it up in her hands and wept over it. 'Oh my darling, if you must die, I will die too!' she said. And she kissed its head.

But when she kissed its head, her lips touched something hard and sharp. It was a pin, and she pulled it out. And the dove opened its eyes. She kissed its head again, and felt another pin, and pulled that out. And the dove cooed. She kissed its head a third time, and her lips touched the third pin, and she pulled that out. And the dove vanished, and there was the prince.

He took her in his arms and said, 'Now we are free for ever more!' And they went back hand in hand to the king's palace.

Then the king pulled down the glass tower, and sent for the simpleton to reward him.

'Choose whatever you like,' said the king to the simpleton.

The simpleton thought for a long time, and then he said, 'I would like a pretty apron for my mother.'

'You shall have a pretty apron for your mother,' said the king, 'but that is not enough. Choose something else.'

The simpleton thought for another long time, and then he said, 'I would like half a bucket of oats for my dear little donkey.'

'Your little donkey shall have its oats,' said the king. 'But choose something for yourself now. Something really costly and splendid.'

The simpleton thought and thought, and then he grinned and said, 'I should like a silver feather to wear in my hat.'

And since he couldn't think of anything else that he wanted, he got his silver feather. He stuck it in his hat, and went home, and showed it to his mother.

'You think I tell lies, mother,' he said. 'But this feather is no lie!'

And he walked about as proudly as if the king had set a gold crown on his head.

6 · The Yellow Dragon

Once upon a time there lived in China a farmer called Yin, who had an only son called Wu. Wu was a silent and dreamy boy; he thought much and spoke little; and perhaps no one understood him but his grandmother, who had brought him up, his mother being dead.

One day, when Wu was thirteen years old, he was sitting at the gate of his father's garden, looking out across the great plain and the mountains that encircled it. A river wound through the plain, and a highway ran by the river. And as Wu sat thinking his dreamy thoughts, he saw a youth on a white horse coming along the highway. The youth was dressed in yellow garments, and four men servants attended him, one of them holding an umbrella over his head, to shield him from the sun.

The youth in the yellow garments rode up to the garden gate, and said, 'Son of Yin, I am weary. May I enter your father's garden, and rest?'

Wu stood up and bowed. 'Enter, my lord,' he said. And he opened the gate.

By this time farmer Yin had seen the stranger and had run to welcome him. The yellow-clad stranger dismounted in the garden, and one of his servants tethered the horse to the gate post. Farmer Yin brought out food and drink, and he and the stranger talked together. But Wu stood with his hands in his sleeves and his arms folded, watching and listening, but saying no word.

And by and by, when the meal was ended, the yellow-clad

stranger stood up, and said, 'Farmer Yin, I thank you for your hospitality.' He bowed, and walked across the garden to where his horse was tethered. He walked through the gate and mounted the white horse, and Wu, who had followed him silently, noticed that as the servant who carried the umbrella passed through the gate, he turned that umbrella upside down.

Before he rode away, the yellow-clad stranger turned to Wu, and said, 'I shall come again tomorrow.' Wu bowed and said, 'Come, my lord!'

Wu stood at the gate and watched the stranger and his four servants moving away and away, until they vanished from sight.

That evening, farmer Yin said to Wu, 'My son, there is something that very much surprises me. That noble youth who honoured us with his presence this afternoon knew my name. But I have never seen him before. Whilst I spent the precious moments in prattling, you were watching the strangers closely. Tell me, did you notice anything unusual about them?'

And Wu answered dreamily, 'The clothes that the strangers wore had no seams. The white horse was covered not with hair but with tiny white scales; and he had spots of five colours under the scales. The hoofs of the horse and the feet of the strangers never touched the ground.'

Said Yin, 'Are you sure of what you say?'

Said Wu, 'I am sure.'

Said Yin, 'Then they were not men, but spirits!'

And Wu spoke dreamily again. 'I watched them as they travelled westward. Rain-clouds were gathering above the mountains. And when the strangers were a great distance off, they all rose into the air, and vanished in the clouds.'

Said farmer Yin, 'My son, I don't know what to make of all this! We must ask your grandmother what she thinks. For your grandmother is very wise.'

The grandmother was fast asleep. She did not want to be disturbed, and they woke her with difficulty, for she was very old. When she had heard their tale, she said, 'The horse was a dragon horse. When spirits appear before human beings they wear magic garments that have no seams. Spirits tread on air, their feet do not touch the ground. As these spirits went westward, they rose higher and higher into the air, going towards the rain-clouds. The noble youth was the Yellow Dragon. He is the one who raises storms; and he had four followers, which are the four winds. The storm will be great. May no evil befall us!'

Wu bowed to the grandmother and said, 'One of the strangers carried an umbrella. And he turned the umbrella upside down before passing through the garden gate.'

'That is a good omen,' said the grandmother. 'But the storm will be great.' And she slept again.

Farmer Yin went to the door of his house and looked up at the sky. Huge black clouds were rolling up from beyond the mountains; they massed and crowded together until they covered the sky from end to end. It became so dark that Yin could not see his hand when he held it up before his eyes. He went in and shut the door. 'I shall sit up all night,' he said.

'With my honoured father's permission, I shall sit up also,' said Wu.

'Yes, yes,' said farmer Yin. 'Only your grandmother, who knows no fear, could sleep on such a night!'

So young Wu lit a candle in a yellow lantern, and put on a yellow robe in honour of the Dragon Youth. And all night he sat quietly reading charms from an old yellow book.

And, with the dawn, came such a storm as no man alive could remember in all his days before. The wind bellowed, rain fell in torrents, thunder pealed continuously, and flash after flash of lightning lit up the swollen streams that poured down from the mountains. The river rose in flood and covered the plain, and wherever the ground was a little higher, the cattle gathered on the shrinking mounds. But through it all, the grandmother slept on.

'Oh, my son, my son, why did we not flee to the mountains?' wailed farmer Yin. 'If the storm lasts much longer we shall be drowned!'

'I do not think we shall be drowned,' said Wu.

But why he thought as he did, he would not say.

All day the storm raged and the floods rose, and by night the farm house was entirely surrounded by deep water.

'We cannot escape now!' cried Yin.

Wu did not answer. And farmer Yin, who was by this time scared out of his wits, took Wu by the shoulder and gave him a little shake. 'What are you thinking, my son?' he cried.

'I was thinking,' said Wu, 'of that upside down umbrella. And I was remembering what the noble Dragon Youth said before he rode away.'

'*What* did he say?' cried farmer Yin. 'My wits are in a turmoil, I can remember nothing!'

'He said, "I shall come again tomorrow." '

'Oh! Oh!' cried Yin, 'and he has come indeed!'

Wu laid down his book and went to the door. He opened the door and looked up at the sky. 'Shut it! Shut it! Shut that door!' cried farmer Yin. 'Are you mad? The water will come in!'

But Wu stood looking up at the sky. The flood was washing at the garden gate; but the water did not flow into the garden. And when Wu felt the door posts, they were dry. So at last he came back into the house and shut the door.

'I have just seen the Dragon,' he said. 'As I looked towards the sky, he spread out his great wings above our home. He is protecting us now.'

'Alas, my son, you are dreaming!' said farmer Yin.

'No, my honoured father, I am not dreaming,' said Wu. 'Listen!'

'What is there to listen to but this howling storm?' cried farmer Yin.

'Listen!' said Wu again. 'There is no rain falling on our roof.'

Then Yin listened, and knew that his son spoke truth. 'This is a great miracle!' he said.

'It was well that you welcomed the Dragon Youth yesterday,' said Wu.

'No, no,' said farmer Yin. 'The credit is all yours, my son. It was you who bade him enter.'

Towards evening the storm lessened. The grandmother woke up. After she had eaten her supper, farmer Yin told her that by a great miracle the roof was dry.

'Miracles are made by manners,' she said, and slept again.

'You should sleep also, my honoured father,' said Wu.

'Yes, I can sleep now, for we are safe,' said farmer Yin. 'Praise be to the noble Dragon Youth!' And he went to his bed.

But Wu lit his yellow lantern, and sat all night in his yellow robes, reading charms out of the old yellow book, in honour of the Yellow Dragon.

In the morning, the clouds drifted away; the rain stopped, and at mid-day the sun shone out. But the water still lay over the plain in a vast lake; the village had been washed away, and the people had fled to the mountains. Only Yin's farm stood where it had always stood, with dry roof and unscathed walls. And the lake came no farther than the garden gate.

So Wu went out and sat at the gate. He looked towards the west, and saw the Dragon Youth in his yellow garments riding over the flood on his white horse, and followed by his four servants. They came silently, making no sound at all; and neither the horse's hoofs, nor the feet of the four servants, touched the water.

When the rider reached the gate, Wu rose and bowed. The rider pulled up his horse. 'I told you I should return,' he said.

Wu bowed again.

'But this time I shall not enter the garden,' said the rider.

'As my lord wills,' said Wu, and bowed again.

Then the Dragon Youth plucked a single scale from his horse's neck and gave it to Wu. 'Keep this,' he said. 'I shall remember you.'

Wu took the scale, and bowed yet a fourth time. And when he raised his head again, the rider and his four servants had vanished.

Wu ran to wake his father, who was still sleeping.

'The storm is over,' he said. 'The Yellow Dragon has returned to his pool, and already the floods are drawing back from the plain.'

They both went to tell the grandmother the good news. She was nodding in her chair, but she suddenly opened her eyes wide, and said to Wu, 'Did the Yellow Dragon give you anything?'

Then Wu opened a little wooden box in which he had put the scale from the horse's neck. And he showed it to the grandmother.

The grandmother looked at it and said, 'When the emperor sends for you, all will be well.'

'Why should the emperor send for him?' said farmer Yin.

But the grandmother was asleep again.

When the water had gone from the plain, the people who had taken refuge in the mountains came down again, and began to build up their ruined homes. They could talk of nothing but farmer Yin's house and garden, and the miracle by which it had been saved from the flood. The men going into the city to buy tools and gear carried the tale with them; and by and by it came to the emperor's ears, and he sent for Yin to learn the truth of it.

So Yin set out to visit the emperor, and took Wu with him.

By the time they reached the emperor's palace it was evening. Farmer Yin told his story from the beginning, and Wu stood silent by his side, holding under his arm the wooden box with the scale from the Yellow Dragon's horse in it. The emperor asked to see the scale. Wu opened the box, and the scale shone so brilliantly that the whole throne room was flooded with light; and though the sun had long gone down, the sky outside was bright as noonday.

'This is indeed a miracle!' said the emperor to Wu. 'And I think the Yellow Dragon – may his lordship be gracious to us! – must have bestowed upon you magical power. You shall not return home, you shall stay here with me as one of my royal magicians.'

So Wu stayed with the emperor. And the emperor was right. When Wu held the scale in his hand, he performed great miracles. He cured all manner of diseases, and caused the emperor's army to win victories over all his enemies. The emperor built him a magnificent house, close to the palace; and Wu sent for his father and the grandmother to live with him. His father looked after the emperor's farmlands. The grandmother slept most of the time. But whenever she did wake up, she said something well worth hearing.

7. *Pepito*

There was once a poor widow who had an only son, called Pepito. Pepito worked all day long in the forest, cutting down wood and binding it into faggots to sell. But it was little enough he earned, and sometimes both he and his mother went short of bread.

One day, as he was going to the forest, Pepito met with a merchant. The merchant was richly dressed, and he smiled on Pepito and bade him good morning. Pepito smiled in return, and said, 'Good morning, sir.' But perhaps, if he had been less simple-minded, he would have noticed something deceitful about that merchant's smile.

Said the merchant, 'I am going on a short voyage. If you will come along with me for a few days, I will give you for wages as much gold as you can carry in your hat.'

It didn't take Pepito any time to say he would go on that voyage! The merchant told him to come to one of the quays of the sea port next morning. And Pepito ran joyfully to tell his mother.

Next morning, his mother gave Pepito her blessing, and he set off for the sea port. The merchant had a whole fleet of ships drawn up along the quay. Pepito got aboard one ship with the merchant, the other ships followed, and they sailed off merrily. The sun shone, a good fresh breeze was behind them, the sails filled, the ships scudded along over the bright water.

'Oh, I do like being on the sea!' said Pepito.

In three days they came to an island; and that island was just one steep mountain rising sheer out of the sea. The sides of the mountain were smooth black rock, which looked as if it had been polished. White clouds drifted across its craggy top; and in and out among the clouds, eagles were wheeling and screaming.

There, under the mountain, all the ships came to anchor in a narrow creek.

Said the merchant to Pepito, 'This is where your work begins. You are to go to the top of the mountain and throw down whatever you find there.'

Said Pepito, 'How shall I get up? There is not a single foothold in those black rocks.'

Said the merchant, 'The eagles will carry you.' He gave Pepito a sword, and sewed him up in a bull's hide. 'When the eagles set you down, you can cut your way out with the sword.'

It was very stuffy in the bull's hide, and Pepito felt rather unhappy. But he comforted himself with the thought of the hatful of gold he was to carry home to his mother. The eagles, smelling the hide, and thinking to get some good fresh meat for their little ones, swooped down, seized the hide in their talons, and carried it up to the top of the mountain with Pepito inside it. Then, as they began tearing at the hide with their beaks, Pepito quickly cut the thongs that bound it, scrambled out, and slashed with his sword in all directions, till the eagles flew off screaming.

Now Pepito could look around him, and he saw that he was standing in a large hollow, overgrown with roses and lilies. How those roses sparkled, to be sure! He thought they were sparkling with myriads of drops of dew. He stooped down to smell them, and what did he see? The roses were strewn over not with dew but with diamonds. Millions and millions of diamonds! And under the rose leaves, and scattered everywhere amongst the lilies, there were sapphires and pearls and rubies, and gold cups, and gold and silver coins and bracelets and anklets and neck ornaments. Pepito stood staring like one in a dream, and forgot all about where he was, or what he had been sent up to do.

Until, far below, and faint and shrill, he heard the merchant calling. Then indeed he came to his senses, and began gathering up the treasure and hurling it down to the foot of the mountain.

He worked at a run; he worked all day until he was exhausted, and still the treasure lay heaped about him – there seemed to be no end to it. As fast as he threw it down, the sailors hurried to pick it up. They loaded the ships with it until the ships were full.

And then what did Pepito see? He saw those ships sail off one after the other. Yes, that wicked merchant was leaving him there on the top of the mountain to perish of hunger and thirst!

Pepito shouted, shouted – no ship turned back. He lay down, wept, beat the ground. To die there! Never to go home, never to see his mother again! Never to take her that hatful of gold!

'You hateful, hateful jewels!' he cried, and struck his fist against a huge sapphire that lay embedded under the lilies at his elbow.

And the sapphire moved under his fist. In a rage he seized it up in both his hands and hurled it from him. What did he see then? He saw a ladder going down and down into darkness. And he saw, far down at the end of the darkness, a tiny light.

Now what should he do? Should he go down, or should he not? Perhaps some terrible demon might be lurking down there under the mountain! But to stay where he was would be certain death, and to go down could be no worse. So, taking up his sword, he began slowly and cautiously to climb down the ladder.

When he came to the bottom, he found himself in a passage of rock, lit by a great ruby hung from its roof. He went along the passage and came out into a beautiful valley, bright with sunshine. There was a stream in the valley, meandering through meadows, and there were flowers everywhere. At the end of the valley was a marble palace, and the gates of the palace were wide open.

'Perhaps they will give me some food,' thought Pepito, and he went in through the gates.

Nobody about! He walked from one grand room to another, and still there was nobody. But in one room, richly furnished and full of mirrors, he found a table with a loaf of bread and a flagon of milk on it. By this time he was famished. So, without if you please or by your leave, he ate and drank.

He had the flagon tipped over his nose to drain the last drops of milk from it, when he heard a mighty whirring and clanging of wings, and in through the open door flew a huge dragon. The dragon was a magnificent fellow: he had golden eyes and a green back and blue wings; he had golden horns on his head, and golden talons on his four feet, and a golden spike at the end of his green tail, and a golden beard under his chin. Pepito had no time to hide, so he just grasped his sword tightly, and looked the dragon full in his golden eyes.

Now, though Pepito couldn't know it, this dragon was a kindly soul. And he was also very lonely, for he had lived under that mountain for three thousand years, and had never had the chance of talking to anyone. So he stood staring back at Pepito, and then he smiled. And, yes, he actually wagged his spiked tail.

'Come to stay?' he said. 'Come to live here?'

'I – I don't know,' said Pepito.

'Oh, do stay!' said the dragon. 'What's your name?'

'Pepito.'

'I haven't got a name that I know of,' said the dragon sadly. 'You see, there's no one to call me anything. And no one to talk to except the fishes in the stream. And they're so silly – they do nothing but giggle. You've no idea what it's like being me – no mother, no father, no friend, no anything.' And two large silver tears welled up from his golden eyes and rolled slowly down his scaly green cheeks.

'I expect I'm staying for the present,' said Pepito.

Then he remembered having heard that dragons love pearls. And as he had a big one in his pocket, which he had picked up intending to take it home to his mother, he gave it to the dragon. And what did that dragon do but swallow it.

'Oh,' said Pepito, 'I thought you might wear it.'

'So I'm going to,' said the dragon. And in a moment, there was the pearl, neatly fitted into his green neck under his chin, as if it had grown there. 'Do I look very handsome?' he asked, smirking at himself in all the mirrors.

'Yes, I think you do,' said Pepito.

After that, the dragon couldn't make enough of Pepito. He took him all over the palace, and into his treasury, which was fuller of jewels and gold than even the top of the mountain had been. He gave Pepito a magnificent supper, and a bed fit for a prince, and he was up at dawn, with an apron tied over his scales, cooking everything he could think of for breakfast. And after breakfast, he took Pepito for a walk in the flowery meadows, and called to the fish in the stream to tell them he had found a friend.

The fishes put their heads out of the water and gaped at Pepito, and giggled, and swam away.

'They're unfeeling creatures,' sighed the dragon. 'But you *will* stay with me, won't you?'

And Pepito stayed. Somehow the memory of his home and his mother was becoming less and less distinct. It almost seemed as if he had always lived down in this other world, with no company but one friendly dragon. And then, one day, when the dragon was out, and Pepito was wandering about the palace by himself, he came to a little door that he hadn't noticed before, and the door was locked.

'What's inside that locked door?' he asked, when the dragon came in.

'Oh, don't ask me, please don't ask me!' said the dragon.

But that only made Pepito more curious, and he kept on asking, till at last the dragon said, 'I suppose you must go and look. But I think we shall both regret it.'

And he gave Pepito a little golden key.

Pepito went and opened the door. What did he see? Only a pretty garden full of flowers, with a marble cistern in the middle of it, and the sun setting behind the trees at the far end of the garden.

'Well, what a mystery to make about nothing!' thought Pepito.

He was just going out through the door again, when a pigeon, all rosy in the sunset light, came flying over the trees into the garden. The pigeon fluttered to the edge of the cistern: and suddenly it wasn't a pigeon any longer, but a beautiful maiden dressed in a feather robe. The maiden's long golden hair fell all about her; she took off her feather robe and bathed in the cistern – and, oh dear me, no sooner had Pepito set eyes on her than he fell deeply in love. Now he would speak to her, now he would beg her to stay; but she leaped out of the cistern, put on her feather robe, turned into a pigeon again, and flew away.

Pepito went back to the dragon.

Said the dragon, 'I told you so. Now you are sad!'

Said Pepito, 'I am very, very sad. But I am also glad.'

Said the dragon, 'I don't understand that.'

The dragon told Pepito that the maiden's father was a magician, and her mother a witch; that they had turned her into a pigeon for disobedience, and only allowed her to take her own shape when she came to bathe in the cistern. 'And it's silly to fall in love with a pigeon,' said the dragon. 'You ought to have more sense!'

'I will rescue her!' said Pepito.

'Oh well, if you really want to,' said the dragon, 'it's easy enough. You've only to wait till she comes to bathe again, and then take her feathers away. She can't turn into a pigeon without her feathers. But remember her father is a magician, and her mother . . .'

67

'I don't care *what* her father and mother are!' shouted Pepito, and he rushed back to the little door, unlocked it, and went into the garden. There he hid himself behind a bush, and waited.

He waited all night; he waited all the next day. But when the sun was setting behind the trees, the pigeon came again. It fluttered on to the edge of the cistern, and turned into a beautiful maiden. The maiden took off her feathery robe; she stood there in her shift; her long golden hair fell all about her; and Pepito leaped from his hiding place and seized the robe.

'Oh, give it back to me! Give it back!' cried the maiden.

'No,' said Pepito. And he held the robe high above his head.

The maiden began to weep. But Pepito said, 'I love you, why should you weep?'

And the maiden looked at Pepito, and he was a tall, strong youth and very comely. So she stopped weeping and smiled. And Pepito took her by the hand and led her to the dragon.

Said the dragon, 'Oh well, all right, now there are to be three of us.' But he didn't seem very pleased. However, he rummaged in a chest, and brought out some beautiful blue and silver garments, and the maiden put them on. Her long golden hair fell all about her, and she looked, Pepito thought, more beautiful than anything he had ever dreamed of.

'You had better burn those feathers,' said the dragon.

'No,' said Pepito, 'the feather robe is too beautiful to burn. But I shall keep it safely hidden from you,' he said to the maiden.

And the maiden laughed and said, 'I shall never want to put it on again.'

'Now we must get married,' said Pepito. 'But how can we do that with no one to marry us?'

Said the dragon, 'Don't let that worry you.' And he turned himself into a priest and married them; and then he turned back into a

68

dragon again. 'And I hope you won't regret it,' he said, rather sulkily.

Then it was Pepito's turn to laugh.

Pepito and his wife lived with the dragon for a long time, very happily, and they had two children, a boy and a girl.

One evening, when Pepito's wife had the little girl on her lap, and was singing '*Hush a-bye, baby*' to her, Pepito said, 'I've heard that song before.' And all at once he remembered his mother, and became very thoughtful.

The dragon was giving the little boy a ride on his back. He looked at Pepito and said, 'What are you thinking about?'

Said Pepito, 'About something I'd forgotten – my home and my mother.'

Said the dragon, 'Now I suppose you want to go home and see her?'

Said Pepito, 'Yes, I do.'

The dragon's golden eyes filled with silver tears, but he wiped them away with his claw and went into his treasury. He came back with a sack full of gold, and gave the gold to Pepito. 'Can't go empty-handed,' he said gruffly. 'And if you're going, you'd better go quickly. But you'll come back?'

'Yes,' said Pepito, 'I'll come back.'

Said the dragon, 'Turn your face from me and say, "I want to go home." '

Pepito turned his face away. 'I want to go home,' he said.

Then it seemed to him that he fell asleep. When he woke up he and his wife and the two children were standing outside his mother's door. They all four ran into the house, and there was his mother laughing and crying, and hugging them all in turn.

So Pepito and his wife and the two children lived with the mother. Pepito bought a farm with the gold the dragon had given him. He prospered, and they were happy. And by and by it was to

Pepito as if he had never been away, and the memory of the dragon, and of his promise to go back to him, became less and less distinct.

Pepito had even forgotten about the feather robe, which he had given to his mother to hide. But his mother had not forgotten about it. Sometimes, when she was alone, she would take it out of its hiding place, which was at the bottom of a chest under her linen. Then she would lay the feather robe over her knees, and stroke it, and say, 'Oh the pretty feathers, how soft they are!'

One day, when Pepito was away at market, and the mother had taken the feather robe out of hiding, and had it on her knee, Pepito's wife came into the room with the children.

'Let me stroke the feathers too,' she said.

'No, no!' said the mother. 'Pepito will be very angry!'

But Pepito's wife put out her white hand and touched the feathers. And the robe rose off the mother's knees and wrapped itself round the wife, and each of the children was holding a little white feather. And the wife was weeping and crying out, 'Pepito! Pepito! Bid him seek me in *the castles green and the castles red and the five white towers!*' And all at once she and the children turned into three white pigeons, and spread their wings and flew out through the open door, and away and away.

Pepito came home. He was mad with grief. He couldn't eat, he couldn't sleep, he wandered about the farm, calling and calling to his wife. One day he said, 'It's no good, mother! I shall go out of my mind if I stay here. I must go away and search through the world till I find her.' Then he remembered the garden and the cistern where he had first seen his wife. Then he remembered the dragon. 'I will go back to the dragon,' he said. 'Perhaps he can help me.'

He darkened his face and disguised himself as a gipsy lad, and went to the sea port. The merchant was seeking a lad to take with him to the island. He hired the gipsy lad, not knowing it was Pepito, and promised him, as he had done before, a hatful of gold.

So they set sail, and came to the island. And the merchant sewed Pepito up in a bull's hide, and the eagles carried him up to the top of the mountain.

When he had cut himself out of the bull's hide, Pepito didn't waste time listening to the merchant, who was screaming up at him to throw down the treasure. He went straight to the hole where the ladder was, and down the ladder, and through the rock-passage, and out into the flowery valley.

The dragon was looking out for him. Every day, since Pepito had left him, that dragon had stood at the gates of his palace, watching and waiting. Now, when he saw Pepito coming, he rushed to meet him, flying and hopping and turning somersaults in sheer joy. But when he heard Pepito's sad story, he became very sulky and said, 'I'll have to help you, though I don't know why I should. I would much rather you stayed here with me.'

But Pepito said, 'If I do not find my wife, I shall go mad!'

So then the dragon went to his lumber room, and brought out a rusty sword, and an old hat, and the stump of a poplar tree. 'Here you are!' he said to Pepito. 'The hat will make you invisible; the sword, when bidden, will cut down all before it; and if you get astride the poplar it will take you to any place you name. So go on your way, and don't forget me, if you can help it!'

Pepito took the sword, and put the hat on his head. And the dragon cried out, 'Oh dear! I can't see you any more!'

Then Pepito got astride the poplar and said, '*Carry me to the castles green!*' And the poplar rose into the air and carried him away.

The dragon stood at the gate of his palace, and heard Pepito's voice calling out, 'Good-bye! Good-bye!' and his golden eyes filled with silver tears, and the tears rolled down his scaly green cheeks. But he wiped the tears away with his claw, and stamped his

71

foot, and said, 'Such an old fool I am, to care about a lad that cares nothing about me!'

Meanwhile, the poplar had carried Pepito to the *castles green*. There they were, three castles, built of emeralds, and standing on a flat green field. Pepito ran through them all three, calling and calling, but no one answered him. There was nobody there. So he got astride the poplar again and said, '*Carry me to the castles red!*'

And he came to the *castles red*, and there were four of them, built of rubies, and standing on a red hill. He ran through them all, calling and calling. But nobody answered. There was nobody there. So he got astride the poplar again, and said, '*Carry me to the five white towers!*'

The five white towers were built of white marble, and they stood on a white mountain. Pepito ran through the first tower, and he ran through the second tower, and he ran through the third, the fourth, and the fifth. He was calling and calling, but nobody answered him.

Behind the fifth tower was a little yard, filled with cocks and hens and chickens. And in the yard – there was his wife! She was dressed in rags, and she was scattering grain to the hens and chickens; and, strutting about among the chickens, were two little white pigeons.

Pepito shouted; he took off the hat that made him invisible. His wife saw him – and there they were now, in each other's arms. And the two little white pigeons flew up and perched on Pepito's shoulders.

But they had scarcely time to rejoice together when all the doors in the fifth tower began to bang, and there came a great wind which nearly knocked them off their feet, and sent all the chickens whirling about like autumn leaves. Pepito's wife had only just managed to thrust the hat back on Pepito's head and make him invisible, when her father, the magician, came rushing out of the tower, screaming, 'I smell a man!'

'Yes, father,' said she. 'It is my husband, come to fetch me home.'
'Let him show himself, the coward!' shrieked the magician.
'No, father, he is not going to show himself,' said she.

The magician was rushing about, trying to lay hands on Pepito, and Pepito was running about, dodging out of his way: the chickens were whirling like autumn leaves, the cocks were crowing, the hens were cackling. And the two little pigeons were clinging to Pepito's shoulders, with all their feathers ruffled up by the wind, and their tails blowing up and down. But of course the magician couldn't see the little pigeons because, being on Pepito's shoulders, they were just as invisible as his coat.

So, when the magician found that he couldn't catch Pepito, he called out, 'All right, you can take your wife, if by tomorrow morning you have thrown down this mountain and made a flower garden of it.'

And he went back into the fifth tower, and banged all the doors after him, and screeched with laughter; for he thought, 'The fellow can never do that!'

But Pepito's wife led him to a well at the end of the yard, and gave him a tile, and bid him throw the tile into the well. And when Pepito had thrown the tile into the well, a crowd of huge men rose out of it, and began pulling down the mountain. They worked all night, and in the morning the mountain was gone, and the five white towers were standing in a level garden, bright with flowers.

The magician's rage was terrible. He called to his wife, the witch, and the witch came whirling out riding on a dragoness. The witch had a big stick, and she was beating the dragoness on the head with it, and the dragoness was kicking and plunging and trying to throw the witch off her back. But the witch drove her on for all that, and the witch and the magician were chasing the invisible Pepito round and round the poultry yard. It wasn't much good for Pepito to dodge, because whilst he was dodging one of them, he came near to falling into the clutches of the other. So he drew the rusty sword that the dragon had given him, and cried, 'Little sword of mine, cut them down!'

And the sword went *snick*, and the sword went *snack*; and the magician's head rolled in one direction, and the witch's head rolled in the opposite direction. And the two little pigeons, that were clinging to Pepito's shoulders, fluttered to the ground, and turned into his two little children.

'Hurrah!' said Pepito. 'Now all we have to do is to get astride the poplar and go home. And you can go home, too,' he said to the dragoness.

But the dragoness began to cry, and said she didn't want to go home; because her home was at the bottom of the well in the yard, and it was very deep and dark and lonely. So Pepito said, 'Would you like to have a handsome husband and live in a palace?' And the dragoness stopped crying, and said she would like that very much.

So Pepito and his wife and the children and the dragoness all got astride the poplar, and the poplar carried them to the dragon's palace in the flowery valley.

The dragon was standing at the gates of his palace. He looked very thin and unhappy, for he hadn't touched a morsel of food since Pepito went away. He wanted to die before his time, did that poor dragon. But when he saw Pepito, he rushed to meet him, flying and hopping and doing his best to turn somersaults.

'You've come back!' he shouted. 'You've all come back! You won't go away again, will you? You'll all stay with me now?'

'No,' said Pepito, 'we can't do that. But I've brought you a wife, so that you won't be lonely any more.'

The dragon bowed; the dragoness curtsied. They were a handsome couple. He was all green and gold and blue; and she was all pink and silver. They rushed into each other's arms. Pepito and his wife and the children got astride the poplar to fly home. And, glancing down, as the poplar rose into the air, Pepito looked his last on the dragon and the dragoness.

They were dancing hand in hand along by the stream in the flowery valley.

8. Yanni

I will tell you a story about Yanni.

Yanni was walking along a lonely road to visit his sweetheart. And as he passed by a fountain, a dragon sprang out from behind it.

Said the dragon, 'Good morning, good morning, my Yanni, my dinner!'

Yanni trembled and said, 'Good morning, my dragon! Oh please do not eat me!'

But the dragon said, 'I am hungry, my Yanni, I am hungry, my dinner!'

Said Yanni, 'My dragon, my dragon, if your dinner I must be, let me first say good-bye to my dear little sweetheart.'

Said the dragon, 'You shall go on your way to your sweetheart, my Yanni. You shall bid her good-bye for ever and ever, if you swear to come back, for I must have my dinner!'

So Yanni swore he would come back, and he went sadly on his way, and came to the house of his little sweetheart.

Said his little sweetheart, 'Why are you sad, my Yanni, my lover? Do I no longer please you, my Yanni?'

And Yanni said, 'Oh how greatly you please me, my dear little sweetheart! But a dragon I met by the fountain has asked me to dinner.'

Said his dear little sweetheart, 'Where you go, Yanni, I will go with you.'

But Yanni said, 'Where I am going, no maid shall go with me.'

Said his little sweetheart, 'I will cook you a dinner, my Yanni, my lover. I will shake up your mattress, and spread out your blanket.'

But Yanni said, 'Where I am going, my dear little sweetheart, no maid shall go with me. There is no cooking, nor eating, nor spreading of mattress, nor sleeping in that place.'

And his little sweetheart said, 'Yet I will go with you, Yanni, my lover. Our love will protect us.'

So the two of them set out, like two pretty doves that fly into the fowler's net.

And there was the dragon leaning against the fountain.

When the dragon saw them walking towards him, he cried out, 'My dinner, my dinner! My dinner comes double!'

And when Yanni heard this, he said, 'Did I not tell you, my dear little sweetheart, that you should not have come here?'

But his dear little sweetheart said in a loud voice, 'Go on, go on,

my Yanni, my lover! Go on, and fear not. *I have eaten nine dragons for breakfast – I will now eat the tenth one!*'

When the dragon heard this, he trembled and said, 'Pray tell me, friend Yanni, pray tell me, my dinner, whose daughter is that one?'

Then the dear little sweetheart stepped boldly in front of Yanni, and said, 'I am the daughter of Lightning, grand-daughter of Thunder. Move aside, Yanni. *I will flash with my lightning, I will crash with my thunder! I will eat this small dragon!*'

But the dragon flew off. He flew off in haste. And he never came back to eat up friend Yanni.

9. *The Dragon and his Grandmother*

Once upon a time there was a king who gathered a great army and marched off to invade a neighbouring country. The king was mean; he paid his soldiers so little that they came near to starving. And there were three soldiers who got talking together.

Said one of them, 'Let's desert!'

Said the second of them, 'But if we are caught we shall be hanged on the gallows.'

Said the third of them, 'You see that great cornfield? Let us go and hide ourselves under the corn. No one will find us there. The army doesn't march through cornfields. And tomorrow, when it has marched on, we will come out and go back to our homes.'

So they went and hid themselves in the cornfield, and waited for the army to march on.

But the army didn't march on. The king was feasting with his courtiers, and he was greedy, and was enjoying the feast so much that he decided it should last for three days.

The soldiers sat for two days and two nights under the corn. They became very hungry. They ate some corn and the husks stuck in their throats. Their throats were parched; they longed for water.

Said the first soldier, 'If we stay here much longer we shall die of thirst.'

Said the second soldier, 'A quick death on the gallows is better than a slow death from thirst. Let us give ourselves up!'

Said the third soldier, 'No, no, brothers! Let us wait a little longer. Something may turn up.'

And scarcely had he spoken when something did turn up. It was a fiery dragon, who came flying over the cornfield. The dragon's eyes were so bright and burning that they could see through anything. And he saw the three soldiers crouched under the corn.

So the dragon hovered over the corn and said, 'Good morning, my manikins! Who are you, and what are you doing there?'

Said the third soldier, 'We are three soldiers, and because our pay was so small we have deserted from that great army you see encamped over there. Now, if we do not come out of the corn, we shall die of thirst. But if we do come out, we shall be hanged.'

Said the dragon, 'Is that all your trouble? I can pick you up in my claws and carry you over the heads of the army. But a bargain's a bargain. If I do that, you must do something for me.'

'We will do anything!' cried the soldiers.

'I will give you seven years of freedom,' said the dragon. 'At the end of that time I will ask you a riddle. If you can guess it, the bargain is ended. If you cannot guess it, you must be my servants through all eternity.'

Said the soldiers, 'We agree!' What else could they say?

The dragon came down into the corn, and the corn scorched all round him with his fiery breath, and began to blaze. The king's officers cried, 'Someone has set the cornfield on fire! All hands to the water buckets!'

The army was on the move now, every man running with pails of water. But the dragon caught the three soldiers up in his talons and flew with them over the heads of the army, and everyone was so frightened that they dropped their water buckets, and the whole army ran and hid in the tents. And the king, who was still feasting,

swallowed a chicken bone, and had a bad pain for long enough.

The dragon flew with the three soldiers a long way off, and set them down outside a big city.

'Now,' said he, 'you must put your names to our agreement.'

He took a book from his right ear, and a pen from his left ear, and the three soldiers signed their names at the bottom of a page of writing. The writing said all about the seven years of freedom and about the riddle, and about their being the dragon's servants to all eternity if they couldn't guess that riddle.

'Good!' said the dragon. 'That's settled. Now you can go and enjoy yourselves for the present.' And he took a little whip from under his right wing. 'Whip and slash with this,' he said, 'and as much money as you want will jump up before you. You can live like lords, and dress like princes. You can eat like kings and ride about in carriages. But at the end of seven years . . . Ha! Ha!'

And he gave a laugh that set the sky thundering, and spread his wings, and flew away.

The soldiers travelled on merrily with their little whip. They whipped and slashed with it, and with every slash they gave, money came bouncing about them like hailstones. They bought fine clothes, they bought horses, they bought carriages, they travelled from city to city, they lived like lords, and everywhere they went there was feasting and merrymaking. But they were good-hearted fellows; they did no harm to anyone; on the contrary, they gave away money to all who needed it. Yes, that was easy for them to do; but still, they did it. And perhaps the mean old king whom they had served wouldn't have been so generous.

So they lived merrily for six years; and they lived merrily for fifty-one more weeks, and for three more days, and for another day. And then two of them suddenly became scared out of their wits.

Said the first soldier, 'In three more days, what will become of us?'

Said the second soldier, 'That dragon's laugh when he spoke about the riddle – I shall never forget it!'

But the third soldier said, 'Keep up your hearts, brothers! I'll find a way to guess that riddle! I wasn't born yesterday!'

They went into a field and sat down. Two of them had faces as long as fiddles. And an old woman came over a stile into the field, and said, 'Lawks a mercy! What's the matter with you two fine gentlemen? Have you got stomach aches? Or is the hangman at your elbows?'

Said the first soldier, 'It's enough to make anyone's stomach ache!'

Said the second soldier, 'It's worse than any hangman. Hanging would be quick, but this is for eternity!'

Said the third soldier, 'They're crying out before they're hurt, mother.' And he told the old woman all about it.

Said the old woman, 'I think I can help you – if so be you'll help yourselves. You see that little wood over there? Let one of you go into it, and walk on till he comes to a tumbledown sort of little house, built of rocks. If he goes in there he may hear something.' Off she went, across the field, over a stile, and out of sight.

The two melancholy soldiers sat where they were, with their chins on their fists, and their faces as long as fiddles. But the third soldier jumped up.

Said the first soldier, 'Where are you going?'

'Into the wood, to find that little house made of rocks.'

Said the second soldier, 'Much good that will do us!'

But the third soldier laughed and walked off, and came to the little rock house in the wood.

He pushed open the door, and went in. And there was a very old woman sitting on the floor; for there was neither chair nor table in the house. Said she, 'Who may you be?'

'One in need of your help, granny,' said the third soldier. 'And who may *you* be?'

83

'Oh,' said she, 'I'm the dragon's grandmother, that's who I am! But he doesn't treat me right. Would you believe it? He leaves me here without a bed and without a fire, and without a penny piece to call my own!'

So then the soldier slashed with his little whip, and the money jumped about him like hailstones. 'Pick it all up, granny,' said he. 'There's more than penny pieces for you!'

'Oh! Oh! Oh!' The dragon's grandmother scrambled about, picking up the coins; and she hid them away in a big bag she had tied under her petticoat. 'You've a pretty face, laddy, and pretty manners, that I must say!' she said to the soldier. 'And if I can help you, I will.'

So then the soldier told her about the dragon and the riddle.

The dragon's grandmother promised she would do her best to find out the answer for him. She lifted a stone in the floor, and showed the soldier a cellar underneath. 'Hide yourself down there,' she said. 'Don't stir, don't sneeze. But listen like a fox.'

The soldier lowered himself into the cellar, and the dragon's grandmother put back the stone. By and by the soldier heard the clanging of the dragon's wings outside; and he heard the clatter of their scales as the dragon folded his wings, and stamped into the house. He had a sack full of food and a skin full of wine with him, and he flung them down on the floor. And he and his grandmother ate and drank.

'Well, sonny,' said the grandmother, after the dragon had eaten his fill, and was puffing out hot breaths of contentment, 'how many souls have you got your claws on today?'

'Not much luck today,' said the dragon. 'But I've got a tight grip on three soldiers. Got 'em like that!' he said. And he clenched his talons till they sounded like swords clashing together.

'How have you got 'em so tight, then?' said the grandmother.

'Because they have to guess my riddle,' said the dragon, 'or be my servants to all eternity.'

'What if they guess it?' said she.

'They won't guess it,' said he.

'Maybe they will,' said she. 'Riddles *can* be guessed.'

'Not this one can't,' said the dragon.

So then the grandmother said all riddles could be guessed, and the dragon said *his* riddle couldn't, and they got to arguing about it, and the dragon lost his temper, and shouted, 'In the North Sea lies a dead sea-cat – that shall be their roast meat. And the rib of a whale – that shall be their silver spoon. And the hollow foot of a dead horse – that shall be their wine glass. Are you telling me, you old fool, that anyone could guess that?'

'No, I'm not telling you anything of the kind,' said the grandmother. 'You needn't lose your temper.'

'You're enough to put the whole universe out of temper!' said the dragon. 'I'm going to find myself a comfortable bed inside a volcano, and sleep for three days.'

And he went out of the little house, and flew away.

The dragon's grandmother took up the stone in the floor, and called the soldier. Said she, 'Were you hearkening like a fox?'

'Trust me!' said the soldier.

And he slashed with his little whip again, and gave the grandmother another heap of money. 'Good-bye, granny!' said he. 'I'll come and see you again some day.'

'So do,' said she. And the soldier went back to his comrades, and told them the riddle and its answer.

Then they all three began to dance about and shout for joy. They cracked the little whip till the money bounced up from the ground and down through the air; and they spent that money without stint for the next two days.

On the third day came the dragon. He had his book under his wing, and his great jaws were stretched in a tremendous grin.

'Well, well,' said he, 'I see you're merry! And why shouldn't you be? You'll find it hot work serving me to all eternity, but you'll get used to it. Now I'm going to take you down into my volcano. You shall have a fine meal there. But if you can tell me what you will have for your roast meat, then perhaps you needn't come. And, of course, if you don't come, you will keep the whip.'

Then the first soldier said, 'In the North Sea lies a dead sea-cat. That shall be our roast meat.'

The dragon didn't want to believe his ears. He took the grin off his face and gnashed his teeth together. 'That's only the first part of the riddle,' he hissed. 'What shall be your spoon?'

Said the second soldier, 'Do you mean a silver spoon or a metal spoon?'

'A silver spoon, you dolt!' shouted the dragon.

'The rib of a whale shall be our silver spoon,' said the second soldier.

'You're a fool!' growled the dragon.

'But isn't it right?' said the second soldier.

'Of course it's right!' snarled the dragon. And his eyes burned and sparkled, and flames came out of his mouth. Then he gave a laugh that made the skies thunder. 'But it's not the end of the riddle!' he shouted. 'You've got to tell me what shall be your wine glass!'

'The hollow foot of a dead horse, that shall be our wine glass,' said the third soldier. 'But I think we won't dine with you today, thank you all the same.'

The dragon dropped his book and flew away with a loud shriek. And the three soldiers laughed and laughed and laughed. Then they took their little whip and went on their way, and lived richly and merrily to their lives' end.

10 · The Thirteenth Son of the King of Erin

There was a king in Erin who had thirteen sons. And the king asked a wise man what he must do to make all go well with himself and his people. The wise man consulted his magic books, and said, 'Know, O king, that if you would have all go well with yourself and your people, you must give one of your sons to Fate.'

So the king called his sons together, and bid them draw lots to see which should be given to Fate. And the lot fell upon the thirteenth son, whose name was Sean.

The king gave Sean a horse of fleetness and a sword of sharpness, and embraced him, and sent him on his way.

Sean rode until he came into another kingdom, where there were three giants, living in three castles. The first giant thought to make a meal of Sean; but Sean slew him with the sword of sharpness, and took possession of the giant's castle, and of a black dress and a black horse, which he found there.

The second giant, also, thought to make a meal of Sean; but Sean slew him with the sword of sharpness, and took possession of his castle, and of a blue dress and a brown horse, which he found there.

Then the third giant thought to make a meal of Sean. But him, also, Sean slew, and took possession of his castle, and of a dress and a pair of boots and a horse which he found there. The horse was red, and the dress was of as many colours as there are in the sky from dawn to dusk, and the boots were of blue glass.

So, when Sean had killed these giants, and taken possession of these things, he stained his face, that none should know him, and hired himself out as a cowherd to the king of that country. And the country lay along the shore of the sea.

And in the sea there lived a terrible dragon, with a mouth big enough to swallow the world, and with three sharp swords coming out of that mouth. And every seven years this sea dragon must have a maiden for his dinner. The maidens of the country drew lots for which of them should become the dragon's dinner; and this year the lot had fallen on the king's daughter.

The king was going mad with grief; he sent out heralds to summon champions from all the countries round, offering his daughter in marriage to whichever of them would slay the dragon. Hundreds of champions gathered on the shore; but when they saw, far off, the head of the dragon rise above the waves, with his mouth open to swallow the world, and the three sharp swords coming out of that mouth, they all ran away, and left the princess sitting on the shore alone. Then came Sean, dressed in the black dress and riding the black horse which he had taken from the first giant. And the dragon was still afar out to sea. So Sean sat down beside the princess, and fell asleep, with his head in her lap.

And the princess cut three hairs from his head.

But when the dragon came out of the sea to devour the princess, Sean woke and leaped to his feet. With one stroke of the sword of sharpness he cut off the dragon's head. But the dragon rushed back into the shallow water, and the head rushed after him, and gave a jump, and fitted itself on to his body again.

The dragon was sulky. No one had ever cut off his head before. He paddled back into the deep water, and turned his head over his

shoulder, and shouted, 'I won't fight any more today. But I shall be here again tomorrow; and I will swallow the whole world before me as I come!'

And Sean went back to tend his cows, and the princess went back to her father's palace.

The next day the princess sat on the shore again. There was no help for it – she had to give herself to the dragon if her country was to be saved. There were no champions on the shore this time: all the hundreds of them had heard how the dragon's head had been cut off and had fitted itself on to his body again. And they said, 'There is no killing such a monster.' So they all went back to their homes.

Then came Sean, dressed in the blue dress of the second giant, and riding on the brown horse. He sat down by the princess to wait for the dragon, and he fell asleep with his head on her lap. The princess took from her pocket the three hairs she had cut from Sean's head the day before, and laid them out on his forehead, and said to herself. 'It is the same hero in a different dress. May Fate give him the victory!'

Then the dragon's head appeared above the waves afar off, and his great mouth was open, ready to swallow the world, and the three sharp swords in his mouth were flashing in the sun's rays.

'Wake, wake, my hero!' cried the princess. 'The dragon is coming!'

And Sean woke and jumped to his feet and ran into the shallow water to meet the dragon. The dragon reared up his great body that was covered with brown seaweed: he reared up his great body high above Sean, and Sean struck with the sword of sharpness and cut that body clean in two. One half of the body fell to the right of Sean, and one half fell to the left of him; but from left and right the two halves rushed, and joined themselves together.

'Ha, ha! little hero!' roared the dragon out of his enormous mouth. 'I am not so easy to kill as all that! But I shan't fight any more today, so the princess may go home. Tomorrow I will come again, and all the heroes on earth won't save her from me!'

And the princess went back to the palace, and Sean went back to tend his cows. But he thought to himself, 'What can I do? Must I fight this unkillable dragon every day for the rest of my life?'

So that evening he went up to the third giant's castle, to visit the housekeeper there.

The housekeeper said, 'Why are you so solemn? What are you thinking about?'

Sean said, 'I am thinking I do not know how to kill the dragon.'

The housekeeper was grateful to Sean, because he had freed her from the giant and given her the castle to live in. She said, 'Let your sword of sharpness lie in its scabbard. It is no use against such a dragon. Here is something that may help you.' And she gave Sean a little wizened brown apple. 'Throw this into the dragon's mouth,' she said, 'and see what comes of it.'

The next morning the princess sat on the shore again. And Sean came riding on the red horse of the third giant. He was wearing the dress that had as many colours in it as has the sky from dawn to dusk. And he had the blue glass boots on his feet. The princess did not need to look at his hair this time. She knew him at once, and she said to herself, 'Here is my hero again! Perhaps I shall not die today.'

And Sean got off his horse and stood waiting on the shore, and saw the dragon's head lifted above the waves afar off, with his mouth open to swallow the world, and the three swords gleaming. The dragon came nearer and nearer, and the sea boiled about him. And he came into the shallow water, and his great claws stirred up the sand in brown eddies.

'Today I will have her!' he bawled, and all the cliffs echoed with the roar of his voice.

And Sean took thirteen strides back from the edge of the water, and the dragon came out of the sea on to the shore. He opened his huge mouth wide, wide, wider, and the three swords clashed and rang with his rage. And Sean tossed the wizened brown apple into his open mouth; and the dragon toppled sideways and fell on the sand. His great body flattened out and began to melt; and very soon there was nothing left of him but a little dirty brown jelly; and the small waves coming up the shore soon washed that away.

The princess jumped up to embrace Sean, but he leaped on to the red horse and galloped away. The princess tried to cling to him. But all she found herself clinging to was one of his blue glass boots.

When the people heard that the dragon was dead, they danced

and feasted and lit bonfires; and all the bells in all the steeples rang and rang the whole day through. The king sent out his heralds to say that the princess should marry the Dragon Slayer; and the princess was willing enough. But where was the Dragon Slayer? All that the princess had of him was a blue glass boot.

So then the king ordered every unmarried man in the kingdom to come and try on the boot. 'And whomsoever the boot fits,' he said, 'that man shall marry my daughter, and be my heir.'

And there came to the palace old men and young men, and small men and tall men, and all the champions who had fled from the shore on that first morning came hurrying back from their homes far and near. And every man in his turn tried on the boot.

But the boot would not fit any of them. If the man was big, the boot shrunk itself up as small as a toy; and if the man was small, the boot swelled itself till none but a giant could have worn it. Some men cursed the boot, and some men shed tears. But rich man and poor man and champions and all, every man went away disappointed.

The king was at his wits' end, and he sent for a blind sage whom he used to consult in any emergency.

Said the sage, 'Has not your majesty a cowherd?'

'Yes,' said the king, 'I have a cowherd. Why?'

Said the sage, 'Send for him, your majesty.'

So the king sent his servants to summon the cowherd. But the cowherd was not to be found.

Said the sage, 'Was there not a hero who killed the giants of the Three Castles on the Three Hills?'

'Yes,' said the king. 'I believe there was. Why?'

Said the sage, 'Send for him, your majesty.'

So the king sent twenty strong men to summon the hero who had killed the three giants.

The twenty strong men went to the castle of the first giant, and found no one. They went to the castle of the second giant, and found no one. They went to the castle of the third giant, and there was Sean, sitting by the kitchen fire, having dinner with the housekeeper.

Now whether Sean loved the princess much, or whether he loved her little, or not at all, is not known. But certain it is that he did not want to go to the palace. So he seized the twenty strong men and bound them together in a bundle. And then he went on with his dinner.

When the men did not return, the king sent twenty more strong men to summon Sean to the castle. And by the time they arrived at the third giant's castle, Sean had finished his dinner and was out in the orchard, helping the housekeeper to hive a swarm of bees.

'You must drop that work and come to the palace,' said the captain of the twenty men.

But Sean seized these twenty strong men also, and bound them in a bundle. He bound one bundle of men to the other bundle of men. And then he went back to the bees.

And when none of his men came back, the king said to the sage, 'What shall I do?'

Said the sage, 'Go yourself, your majesty.'

So the king went. And the princess sat in the palace with the blue glass boot in her lap, and waited.

The king went to the first castle, and he went to the second castle; and when he came to the third castle, he found Sean in the parlour, playing cribbage with the housekeeper.

'You must come to the palace and try on the boot,' said the king. 'For every other unmarried man in the kingdom has tried, and it won't fit any of them!'

Said Sean, 'I do not want to try on any boot, your majesty. I prefer to go barefoot.'

And he went on playing cribbage with the housekeeper.

93

The king scolded, the king argued, the king pleaded. But Sean would not move. So then the king plumped down on his knees, and besought Sean with tears in his eyes. And the sight of a king on his knees was more than Sean could endure, and he tossed his cards on the table and stood up, and said, 'Very well. I will come.'

And when he said that, the blue glass boot gave a spring off the princess's lap, and a spring through the palace window, and a spring through the air right up to the third giant's castle and into the parlour, and fitted itself on to Sean's right foot. And Sean laughed and said, 'Very well, I will marry the princess. She need not be ashamed of me – I am the thirteenth son of the king of Erin.'

And he told the king all about himself.

Then he undid the bundle of men, and they all went back to the palace together. Sean and the princess were married, and they went to live in the third giant's castle. The housekeeper looked after them well. And when, by and by, the princess had twin sons, the housekeeper was made head nurse. And that was a proud day for her.

11 · Baskets in a Little Cart

Once upon a time there was an empress in China who wanted her son to be heir to the throne. But the emperor had an older son by a former wife. The name of this son was Chu-ti. And the empress hated Chu-ti with all her heart, and wanted to get rid of him.

So one day she said to the emperor, 'If Chu-ti is to inherit this great empire, it is time he learned something about government. Send him to the province of Ho-hi-to, and let him govern there for a few years.'

'Ho-hi-to,' said the emperor. 'Where is that?' For his empire was so vast that he didn't know anything about half of it.

'Ho-hi-to lies to the south,' said the empress. 'It is a magnificent and flourishing province.'

'Ah, if that is so, by all means let Chu-ti go and govern it,' said the emperor. And he sent Chu-ti off to the province of Ho-hi-to with a small following of noble youths.

On his way to the province, Chu-ti met with a priest.

Said the priest, 'All hail, and long life to your excellency!'

Said Chu-ti, 'All hail, and long life to you, O priest!'

The priest took a sealed packet out of his sleeve. 'In this packet,' he said, 'are three sheets of paper. If you should find yourself in perplexity, open the packet and read. But do not read more than one sheet at a time.'

So Chu-ti took the sealed packet from the priest and thanked him. And he and the priest went their separate ways.

95

Chu-ti was looking forward to governing the magnificent and flourishing province of Ho-hi-to. But when he got there, what did he find? He found only a barren wilderness, with just a few huts scattered here and there, and some poor, ragged people scratching up the soil for a livelihood.

'Oh, what a place my father has sent me to!' cried Chu-ti.

And he sat down on the ground with his arm before his face. And the noble youths gathered round him.

'Let us turn our horses and ride home!' they said.

'No!' said Chu-ti. 'No! This is my stepmother's doing. It was her wish that we should perish in this wilderness. If we go back she will devise some new mischief. But what to do in this perplexity, I do not know.'

Then he remembered the sealed packet which the priest had given him, and he took it from his bosom and opened it, and read the first sheet. This is what was written on it:

'Where the wilderness appears,
There the prince a city rears.'

And under these words was a plan of the city, with streets and palaces and temples and towers, all drawn neatly to scale.

And Chu-ti took heart, and summoned the poor people out of their huts, and began to build the city. The noble youths, too, worked with a will. In the course of time they reared a magnificent city, with streets, palaces, temples and towers all according to the plan. The fame of the city spread, and people came from the east and from the west, from the north and from the south – merchants and great lords and craftsmen and labourers – to live in the city. Chu-ti found himself governing a great and prosperous province.

Such was the crowd of people that by and by they had drunk up all the water supply. The water diviners went round with their rods seeking for new springs; but they only found little trickles of water, and very soon all the little trickles of water were drunk up also.

Here was a perplexity indeed! Chu-ti thought of the packet the priest had given him, and he opened it and took out the second sheet of paper. This is what was written on it:

'Neither north, south, east, but *west*,
There find water of the best.'

So Chu-ti ordered his workmen to go and dig at the west end of the city.

The workmen were digging and digging. But they didn't find any water. The diviners stood round with their rods, and the rods didn't bend. And the diviners said, 'There is no water here, my lord Chu-ti.'

But Chu-ti said, 'Dig deeper! Dig deeper!' And every day he said, 'Dig deeper!'

The workmen grumbled, but still they went on digging. And, at a very great depth, and under layers and layers of rock, they at last struck a spring. And the released waters of the spring bubbled up clear and fresh and sparkling to form a well. It was such a huge well that it supplied all the city.

But you must know that in their deep digging, the workmen had broken into the roof of a dragon's cave. The dragon and his wife had lived in that cave for myriads of years. And when his cave was broken into, the dragon's wrath was terrible. He roared, and he spat, and he breathed out flames. He beat his head against the sides of his cave. He even clawed his poor wife, and made her nose bleed, though it was none of her doing.

'We will leave this miserable city!' he yelled. 'We will go and live far away from these busybodying manikins! But we will have our revenge! We will take all their water away with us! We won't leave them a drop to drink – no, not one drop!'

97

So the dragon changed himself into an old man, and he changed his wife into an old woman, and he came before Chu-ti trembling and bowing, and said, 'My lord Chu-ti, we are your humble servants, and we live in your admirable city. But we are getting old, and we have a daughter in the next province who loves us, and will take care of us. Will you give your humble servants leave to go and live with their daughter?'

'By all means go,' said Chu-ti, 'if that is your wish.'

'It is a long journey, my lord Chu-ti,' said the old man who was the dragon in disguise. 'Will my lord give his gracious permission for us to carry with us a little water from the well, that we may not perish of thirst on the way?'

'By all means,' said Chu-ti. 'Take as much as you can carry.'

And the old man and the old woman left the city.

But that evening, when the people went to fetch water from the well, they noticed that the water had shrunk. The next morning it had shrunk still lower, and by evening the well was dry. They peered into the well, and saw nothing but the dry rock walls going down and down and out of sight. And they ran to Chu-ti clamouring out, 'The water has gone! The water has gone! The well is dry!'

'The well cannot be dry!' said Chu-ti.

The people begged him to go and see for himself. And he went and looked into the well, and saw nothing but the dry rock walls, going down and down, a tremendous way down, and out of sight.

What was to be done? In his perplexity Chu-ti thought of the packet the priest had given him. And he opened the packet and took out the third paper. This is what was written on it:

'Baskets in a little cart –
A prince's wits must needs be smart.'

Chu-ti didn't know what to make of these words. He puzzled his wits, and he puzzled his wits, but still he could make nothing of them. So he sent a herald round the city asking if anyone had seen a little cart with baskets in it.

Nobody had. The herald was returning without any news, when a girl, who lived by the east gate, said, 'Why yes. At noon yesterday I saw an old man and an old woman go out through the gate pushing a little cart with two baskets in it. They took the road to the east.'

The herald went back and told Chu-ti. And Chu-ti mounted his great black horse, and galloped out of the city on the road to the east.

The road stretched away and away over a seemingly endless plain. For a long time Chu-ti galloped without seeing anybody. Then he spied a little cloud of dust on the road ahead of him. When he came up with that little cloud of dust, he saw the old man and the old woman hurrying along as fast as they could, with a little cart between them. The old man was in front, dragging the cart by a rope, and the old woman was behind, pushing the cart; and they were both puffing and panting as if the little cart was very heavy. And on the cart were two baskets.

Chu-ti called to them to stop, and said, 'What are you carrying in those baskets?'

'Just a few ragged clothes, my lord Chu-ti,' said the old man.

But Chu-ti noticed that the sides of the baskets were wet. And he said, 'How is it that the baskets are wet, since no rain has fallen?'

'Oh my lord, we are old and sad. We have shed many tears,' said the old man.

> '*Baskets in a little cart –*
> *A prince's wits must needs be smart.*'

Chu-ti was remembering the words on the paper.

'Open the baskets,' he said.

99

'Oh no, my lord, oh no!' cried the old man and the old woman together. 'It is not for your illustrious eyes to gaze upon our rags!'

'I must and will know what is in those baskets!' said Chu-ti.

And, since neither the old man nor the old woman would open them, he leaned from his horse and thrust his spear first through one of the baskets, and then through the other.

The old man shrieked, and the old woman shrieked, and Chu-ti himself was confounded. For water was pouring out of the baskets. It poured out and it poured out, and never stopped pouring out. Very soon Chu-ti's horse was standing in a big pool, and still the water was pouring out of the baskets. The water became a mighty flood; it was lapping about the horse's hocks, and Chu-ti swung his horse round and galloped before the flood back towards the city. The old man and the old woman had disappeared, and the cart had disappeared; but glancing over his shoulder, and up at the sky, where dark clouds were gathering, Chu-ti saw two mighty dragons with red wings, flying eastward under the clouds.

On and on he galloped; the flood waters were all about him, and in the distance the city stood like a diminishing island, with the water filling the streets, and the people clambering up on to the roofs of their houses. And at the feet of the galloping horse, one of the baskets was rushing through the water faster than the fastest swimmer.

As Chu-ti reached the city, the gates fell down with a crash. The horse reared and whinnied, but Chu-ti urged it on, and it plunged into the flooded streets and swam, with the basket bobbing at its heels. Chu-ti scarcely knew where he was going or what he was doing; but all at once he heard someone calling him, and looking up, he saw the priest who had given him the packet, standing on the highest step of the tallest temple. The priest had a line in his hand with a hook at the end of it, and as the basket came whirling along in the flood, he caught it with the hook and swung it up.

There was the basket now, swinging on the end of the hook above the water; and the priest, in a loud voice, was reciting spells in a strange tongue. The basket swung and swung on the hook, and then it hung still. And as it stopped swinging, the water stopped flowing: the flood went back from the streets, and the people clambered down from the roofs.

The water went back from the city, it went back from the plain; the dark clouds went back from the sky, and the sun shone out. And the priest took the basket off the hook and dropped it down before the temple. It fell deep into the ground, and from the ground a fountain of clear sparkling water sprang up. And from the midst of the fountain rose a pagoda that lifted and fell with the water, floating on the top of it like a ship on the sea. And from the pagoda a glistening spire thrust up, high, high above the city, and the spire swayed with the movement of the water like a ship's mast in a storm. The fountain was a marvel to behold, and it never ran dry. For the waters, that the dragons had thought to carry off, had returned into the heart of the city.

So the people took stones and cast them into the dragon well, and closed it up.

12· The Prince with the Golden Hand

There was once a princess with hair of shining gold, and of exceeding beauty. And because her parents were fearful lest harm should befall her, they kept her shut away from the world until the time came for her to marry. Then the king sent out his heralds to invite suitors for her, and princes and nobles came by the score. They were all young and handsome and brave. And the king said to the princess, 'Choose which you will.'

The princess said, 'I will choose tomorrow. But give me this one day of freedom. Now that I am so soon to be married, surely I am old enough to run and play in the garden by myself?'

The king said, 'Go, my darling,' and the princess ran out, singing. But she hadn't been in the garden for more than a few minutes when a dragon, who was flying overhead, caught sight of her shining golden hair; and he whirled down through the garden like a hurricane, and carried her off.

The king tore his hair. The queen went from one fainting fit into another. But when the king had come to his senses a little, he sent his heralds out again, offering half his kingdom, and the princess's hand in marriage, to whomsoever should find her and bring her back.

Among those who set out to look for the princess were two

brothers, the sons of a neighbouring king. These two princes set off in the summer time, and they travelled through the autumn and through the winter, and through the next spring, and they visited many countries, but nowhere could they get any news of the princess, or of the dragon. So they travelled for another year, and then they came to a wild country in the very middle of the world.

In front of them was a high mountain, and they left their horses at the bottom of the mountain and began to climb on foot. 'For we must leave no place unsearched,' they told each other. They climbed and they climbed, and they came near to the top of the mountain. And there, towering above them, on the very peak of the mountain, they saw a silver palace which was balanced on a cock's foot. And at one of the windows, they saw a maiden sitting with her back to them, and her hair shone more brightly gold than the sun itself.

'That must be the princess!' they cried. And though the way was very steep and very rocky, they both began to run. As they ran, they saw the silver palace spinning round and round at a violent rate, and there came such a fierce wind from the top of the mountain that they were both knocked flat. They had scarcely scrambled to their feet, or recovered their breath, when the wind turned to a frost so intense that their breath began to freeze: the mountain became a sheet of ice, the princes fell frozen to the ground, and the snow came and covered them.

And that was the end of their seeking.

Back in the kingdom from which the princes had set out, their father, the king, and their mother, the queen, waited and waited for news of their sons. They waited one year, they waited two years, they waited three years. And then the king said to the queen, 'We shall never see our sons again.'

But still the queen hoped on. And whenever travellers came that way, she sent for them, and asked if anywhere in their journeying they had met with two gallant young princes riding on dappled horses with trappings of gold. But always they said 'no'; and always she sent them on their way with a present, and said, 'Pray for my sons.'

Then, one day, the two dappled horses with trappings of gold came home, and their saddles were empty. But still the queen would not give up hope; until at last there came to the palace a hermit with a long white beard, who was travelling from one holy place to another. Of him, also, the queen asked if anywhere in his journeying he had seen the two princes, and he answered 'no'. Then she would have made him a present, but all he would take was a handful of raisins. And the queen gave him the raisins, and said, 'Pray for my sons.'

'Your sons are dead,' said the hermit. 'My prayers will not avail them. But you shall have another son, the like of whom the world has never seen.'

And he bade her be comforted, and left her.

Some time after this, the queen did have a baby boy, and the baby was born with a hand of gold. And when he was three days old, he got out of his cradle, and spoke.

'Mother,' he said, 'why are you sad?'

And the queen told him about his brothers.

Said he, 'I will find my brothers!' And he toddled out into the garden, and bathed in the morning dew. He went out a baby, but he came in again a strapping great boy.

The boy grew from hour to hour. At the end of a month he could wield a sword. At the end of two months he was riding on horseback. At the end of three months he was fully grown. His hair was gold, his right hand was gold, and he had a moustache of pure gold.

'Now I will go out into the world and seek my brothers,' he said.

And he bade his parents good-bye, and set off.

When he had been riding many days, he came to a field of poppies, and on the other side of the field of poppies was a cottage balanced on a cock's foot. Beyond the cottage was a dense thicket, and the cottage had its back to the poppy field, and its front all tangled up in the thicket.

The poppies were giving out a strong, sleepy smell that made the prince yawn, and when he began riding over the field, he could scarcely keep awake. But he set his horse at a gallop, and drew his sword and cut off the poppy heads as he galloped. And so he got across the field.

And there was the cottage with its back to him, and its front tangled up in the thicket.

But Prince Gold Hand said:

> '*Turn, cottage, turn,*
> *On thy cock's foot turn thee;*

With the trees at thy back,
Let thine open door face me.'

And when he said those words, the cottage gave a loud creak, and turned round, and its door opened wide.

So Prince Gold Hand went in through the door, and found a wrinkled old crone, sitting spinning. On one side of her was a beautiful young girl, weaving at a loom; and on the other side of her was a beautiful young girl, embroidering a petticoat.

Said the old crone, 'Good morning to you, Prince with the Moustache of Gold, Hero with the Golden Hand. What brings you here?'

'I am seeking my brothers,' said Prince Gold Hand. And he told her how they had ridden away before he was born, to look for the princess with the hair of glittering gold.

'Pooh!' said the crone. 'Your brothers must have perished long ago, on the mountain that touches the clouds. For it is to the top of that mountain that the dragon carried the princess.'

Said the prince, 'Where can I find this mountain and this dragon?'

'If you take my advice, you won't look for him,' said the crone. 'He would swallow you like a fly! I have not been out of this cottage for a hundred years for fear he would carry *me* off. Eh dear! I was a pretty girl a hundred years ago!'

'He won't want to carry me off,' said the prince. 'I am not pretty. And as for swallowing me – he will get a blow with this gold hand of mine before he does that!'

The old crone began to rock herself and whimper. 'Eh dear, eh dear, what a pretty girl I was a hundred years ago! Hark'ee, Hero with the Golden Hand, if I help you, will you promise to bring me a bottle of the Water of Youth to give me back my beauty?'

'If I can find it, I will bring it,' said Prince Gold Hand.

'You'll find it, oh, you'll find it!' said the crone. 'On the top of the mountain there are four wells. The first is the Heroic Well that

Makes Strong. The second is the Well that Revives. The third is the Well that Restores. The fourth is the Well that Makes Young. Fill me a bottle from this fourth well, and see me skip and dance!'

Then the crone gave the prince a pincushion to throw in front of him. 'That will lead you to the mountain,' she said. 'But when the dragon is not at home, the mountain is guarded by his father and his mother. His mother is the hot South Wind that will shrivel you to a cinder. His father is the cold North Wind that will freeze you to an icicle. Here is a heat-giving hood that will protect you from the one; and here is a flagon of cooling drink which will save you from the other.'

So Prince Gold Hand took the pincushion, and the heat-giving hood, and the cooling flagon, and thanked the old crone, and went on his way. He threw the pincushion in front of him, and it whizzed through the air so fast that he had to gallop to keep up with it. By and by he came to a green valley with a great mountain towering over it. And the pincushion began going up the mountain. So the prince left his horse to graze in the valley and go home when it would, and hastened after the pincushion.

When he had clambered half-way up the mountain, there came such an icy wind that the trees cracked, and the prince's breath began to freeze. But he put on the heat-giving hood, and clambered on, for he found himself snug and warm. The pincushion was still skipping along through the air ahead of him; but all of a sudden it began to hover, and after turning slowly round once or twice, it came to rest on a small snow-covered mound.

Prince Gold Hand scraped away the snow from the mound, and there he saw the frozen bodies of two handsome young men, whom he guessed must be his brothers. He was kneeling down to say a prayer over them, when he saw that the pincushion was skipping up the mountain again. So he scrambled to his feet and hastened after it.

He was near the top of the mountain, when there came such a scorching hot wind that every flower and bush and blade of grass shrivelled into nothingness; the very ground split open, and the prince came near to fainting. But he snatched off his heat-giving hood, and took a deep drink from the cooling flagon, and was instantly refreshed. So he climbed on to the top of the mountain.

The pincushion gave a dip and a twist, and skipped into the prince's pocket. It was leading him no farther.

The prince stood still. In front of him was the great silver palace, balanced on a cock's foot; and out of one of the windows leaned a princess whose hair glittered more brightly than the sun. But the palace had its back to the prince, and between him and it gaped a deep black chasm, going down and down and down into the earth. No man, no hero even, could leap that chasm. So the prince called out in a loud voice:

> '*Turn, palace, turn,*
> *On thy cock's foot turn thee!*
> *Let thy porch bridge the chasm,*
> *And thine open doors face me!*'

Immediately the palace turned with a loud whistling sound: the great jutting portico, with its silver pillars and flight of silver steps, entirely bridged the chasm, and behind the portico the palace doors stood wide open.

And so the prince got safely across the chasm, and went up the steps and through the open doors of the palace, and came into a hall that was made entirely of mirrors. The floor was a mirror, the ceiling was a mirror, and the four walls were four huge mirrors. Over the floor, and through the ceiling, and out of the walls, the prince saw scores and scores of princesses, with glittering golden hair, holding out their hands and running to meet him. But it was only one princess, really, and the rest were her reflections; and when she came close to him and clasped his arm, he knew which was the real princess and which were the reflections.

'Fly! Fly!' cried the princess. 'The dragon is coming! He is terrible, no man can withstand him! He will kill you with one glance of his eyes!'

'I have not come so far, only to turn back now,' said Prince Gold Hand. 'If he kills me, I can but die. But I do not think he will kill me.'

Then, because he was thirsty, and his cooling flagon was empty, he asked the princess for water; and she took a bucket and filled it at the Heroic Well. The prince drained the bucket dry, and she ran and filled it again. And again he drank it dry. If he had been strong and mighty before, he was a hundred times more strong and mighty now that he had drunk that water. He sat down on an iron chair to wait for the dragon. And the chair broke under him into a thousand pieces.

Then he fetched the chair in which the dragon used to sit. The chair was made of the strongest steel in order to hold the dragon's weight. But when the prince sat in it, the chair groaned and creaked and bent under him. One leg of the chair was just about to break, and the prince had just jumped up again, when there came a horrible whistling sound, and the palace spun round and round: every door flew open, and in burst the dragon, riding on a winged horse. The dragon shot fire from his nostrils and flame from his eyes, and out of his great mouth poured clouds of smoke; his body was the body of a giant, covered with sharp scales; his legs were the legs of a tiger, his feet were taloned like an eagle's, and his tail ended in a snake's head, dripping venom. He leaped upon the prince with a roar that set the palace rocking. But the prince stepped aside, thrust his golden hand into the dragon's great gaping mouth, seized him by the tongue, and dashed him against the wall.

The dragon lashed with his tail and clawed with his talons; the glass wall cracked from end to end, and the dragon's head went through it; but still Prince Gold Hand held him by the tongue, and shook and shook, till he shook the life clean out of him.

Then the prince took three bottles and went to the wells, and filled the bottles in turn with the Water that Revives, the Water that Restores, and the Water that Makes Young. And, after that, he put the princess up on the winged horse and got up behind her, and they flew down the mountain to the place where his brothers lay frozen. He sprinkled them with the Water that Revives, and they opened their eyes. He sprinkled them with the Water that Restores, and they sprang up whole and well. And then the four of them got upon the winged horse, and flew to the old crone's cottage.

The cottage had its back to them, and the front of it was again tangled up in the thicket. So Prince Gold Hand said:

> *'Turn, cottage, turn!*
> *On thy cock's foot turn thee:*
> *With the trees at thy back,*
> *Let thine open door face me!'*

And the cottage gave a loud creak, and turned round; and its door opened wide.

So Prince Gold Hand, and his two brothers, and the princess all went into the cottage; and there was the wrinkled old crone at her spinning wheel; and at one side of her was the beautiful young girl weaving at a loom; and on the other side of her was the beautiful young girl embroidering a petticoat. And when the old crone saw Prince Gold Hand she leaped from her stool and croaked out, 'Have you got it? Have you got it?'

'Yes,' said the prince, 'I have got it.'

And he gave her the bottle of the Water that Makes Young, and she seized it in her wizened hands and poured the water over herself, and immediately turned into a beautiful maiden, only less beautiful than the princess herself because her hair did not glitter more brightly than the sun.

And this beautiful maiden curtsied to Prince Gold Hand and said, 'What can I give you as a thank offering? Ask what you will, it is yours.'

But the prince could not think of anything to ask for. The princess with the glittering golden hair was all he desired in the world, and she was already standing with her hand in his. So he turned to his brothers and said, 'What shall we ask for?'

Said his eldest brother, 'If it were left to me, I would ask the young lady at the loom for her hand in marriage.'

Said the middle brother, 'And if it were left to me, I would ask the young lady who is embroidering for *her* hand in marriage.'

Said the beautiful maiden who had been the old crone, 'Well take them! By their smiles I can see they are willing. And now that I am young again, I can't be bothered with grown-up daughters. So now I will wish you good-day!'

And with that, she gave another curtsey – and vanished from their sight.

And the three princes, and the princess with the glittering golden hair, and the two beautiful young girls, all got upon the back of the winged horse, and he flew with them to the palace of the king and queen who were the parents of the princess.

The king and queen were in mourning for their daughter, for they had given up all hope of seeing her again. But when the winged horse with its six riders came down at the palace gates, and they caught sight of that golden hair that glittered more brightly than the sun, their mourning was turned to tears of joy. They wanted to arrange for the marriage of the princess and Prince Gold Hand that very day.

But the princess said, 'There is just one difficulty. When I was carried off by the dragon, he wished to marry me, so I made a vow that I would wed no one who could not guess three riddles I would put to him. The dragon could never guess the riddles, and so I was spared. But a vow is a vow, and a princess must keep it.'

'Ask!' said Prince Gold Hand. 'The riddles would indeed be hard that I could not guess to win you!'

Said the princess gently, 'They are not so very hard. The first one is this: "It walks without feet, beckons without hands, and moves without a body".'

'I think,' said Prince Gold Hand, 'that it must be your shadow?'

'You are right,' said the princess. And she smiled. 'The second riddle is this: "It has four legs, but it is not an animal. It is provided with feathers and down, but it is not a bird. It has a body, and it gives warmth, but it is not alive".'

'I think,' said Prince Gold Hand, 'that it must be your bed?'

'You are right,' said the princess. And she laughed. 'The third riddle is the easiest, and he who guesses it shall be my bridegroom. This is the riddle:

> *"I tie it up; it goes a-roaming;*
> *I loose it, and it stays a-homing".'*

'I think,' said Prince Gold Hand, 'that it must be your shoe?'

'You are right,' said the princess. And she clapped her hands, and turned up her lovely face, and kissed Prince Gold Hand on the lips.

So then Prince Gold Hand sent a courier on the winged horse to take a message to the king and queen who were his parents, and to bring them back on the horse to the weddings of himself and his elder brothers. And for this king and queen, too, the news turned mourning into gladness. The three weddings were held with such splendour and rejoicings as the world had never seen before; and the three princes and their wives lived happily ever after.

13. The Three Dogs

Once upon a time there was an old shepherd who had two children, a boy and a girl. When the time came for the shepherd to die, he said, 'My children, you know I am poor, and I have nothing to leave you but this little house and my three sheep. When I am dead, divide these between you. But, whatever you do, love one another, and don't quarrel over my poor possessions.'

When the shepherd was dead, the brother and sister wept over him, and gave him the best burying they could with their scanty means. And then the brother, whose name was Mario, said, 'Sister, which would you like best to have, the sheep or the little house?'

'I would like best to have the little house,' said the sister.

So Mario took the three sheep, and set out into the world to seek his fortune.

He hadn't gone very far when he met a man followed by three black dogs.

Said the man, 'Good morning, friend! Will you exchange your sheep for my dogs?'

Said Mario, 'I think not. My sheep can at least feed themselves. But where could I find food for three great dogs?'

'All the same you would be wise to take them,' said the man. 'They are not ordinary dogs. This one, the youngest of them, is called Salt. And whenever you feel hungry she will bring you food. The second one is called Pepper, and he will tear to pieces whoever should offer to hurt you. And this huge fellow here is called

Mustard – just look at his teeth and jaws! They can eat through iron and steel as if it were paper.'

Said Mario, 'If what you tell me is true, I should be foolish not to take them. But why should you wish to exchange three such valuable animals for three ordinary sheep?'

'That is my own affair,' said the man. 'Take my dogs then, and good luck to you!' And as he said this, he vanished, and the three sheep vanished. And Mario was left standing with the three dogs.

'Was he a saint, or an angel, or a magician?' thought the astonished Mario. 'At any rate we will put his words to the test.' He turned to the smallest of the dogs and said, 'Salt, I am hungry!'

And no sooner were the words out of his mouth, than Salt disappeared, and re-appeared next moment carrying a basket filled with delicious things to eat and drink.

Mario sat down and ate and drank; and so much did that basket hold that when he had eaten his fill there was plenty of food left over to give to the dogs. He emptied the basket before them, and the dogs ate up everything. And then the basket disappeared, and Mario went on his way with thankfulness in his heart.

By and by, when he was sitting down to rest again, he saw a coach coming along the road. The coach was black, the horses were black, and the coachman was dressed in black. And in the coach sat a pretty girl, dressed in black, and sobbing like one whose heart was broken.

Mario jumped up and hailed the coach, and the coach stopped.

'Where are you going?' he asked the coachman. 'And why are you dressed in black, and why is the lady weeping so bitterly?'

Said the coachman, 'What business is it of yours?'

Said Mario, 'Perhaps no business at all. But I cannot see such grief unmoved, and if I can do anything to help, I will.'

The coachman only grunted – he was a surly fellow. But the girl leaned out of the coach, and the tears were streaming from her eyes.

'O kind stranger, get you gone, and take another road!' she cried. 'This is the road that leads to death. You see that high mountain in front of us? That is the mountain of death. And it is there that I must go to meet my fate. It is there that I am to be devoured by a fiery dragon. For every year he demands the sacrifice of one of the maidens of my father's kingdom. This year it is my turn. And a princess knows her duty.'

She bade the coachman drive on towards the mountain. Mario, with his three dogs, followed the coach. The princess leaned from the window and called to him, 'Go back! Go back!'

But he would not go back.

When they came to the foot of the mountain, the coachman pulled up, and the princess got out. Said the coachman to Mario, 'You are a fool if you stay here another minute!' Then he turned the horses and drove quickly away. But the princess began to climb the mountain, and Mario, with his three dogs, followed her. Every now and then the princess would stop and beseech him to go away. But Mario still followed.

They were not more than half-way up the mountain when they heard a dreadful roaring. The sky above them turned into flames, and down through the flames swooped the dragon in a blaze of fire. The poor princess fell fainting, but Mario stood his ground, and when the dragon alighted on a rock, Mario cried out, 'Now, Pepper, show your mettle!' And Pepper leaped upon the dragon and seized it by the throat.

The dragon clung with its claws to the rock, and beat at Pepper's body with its spiked wings. The rock grew red hot round them, and the dragon's breath sent out clouds of steam and fiery bubbles. But Pepper hung on to the dragon's throat. The dragon writhed and squirmed; Pepper's body was tossed this way and that way, and up and down, like a flag in a gale; but never for one moment did he loose his grip on the dragon's throat. And the dragon's struggles grew weaker and weaker, and the steam of his breath grew thinner and thinner. And by and by he rolled over, stone dead.

And there was Salt licking the princess back into consciousness. And there was Pepper gobbling up the dragon's flesh as if he hadn't had a meal for a week. And there was Mustard, grinding up the dragon's bones with his great jaws. Very soon the princess was standing up and shedding tears of thankfulness; and very soon there was nothing left of the dragon but two of its teeth, which Mario picked up and put in his pocket.

The princess wanted Mario to come back with her to the palace. 'For I think the king, my father, will reward you richly,' she said. She didn't say that the king would also give Mario her hand in marriage; though in her heart she knew it, and was glad.

But Mario said, 'I set out to see the world, and as yet I have seen but little of it. So I will go on my way. But in three years I will return.'

'Is that a promise?' said the princess.

'It is a promise,' said Mario.

And away he went over the mountain and down on the other side of it, with his three dogs following him.

Now the coachman had pulled up at a safe distance, away along the road, to watch the fight. And when he saw the princess walking back towards him alone, an evil thought entered his surly mind. The princess got into the coach, and they drove on until they came to a broad river, crossed by a bridge. In the middle of the bridge, the coachman pulled up the horses, got down, and went to the coach window.

Said he to the princess, 'A fine champion you found, who left you without so much as a word or a sigh! Now *I* have a heart which beats for you alone. It would be worth your while to make a fellow happy. So when I tell the king, your father, that it was I who killed the dragon, you'd better not contradict me. It's no good your scowling at me, my beauty! If you don't promise to agree that it was I who killed that dragon, I shall throw you into the river and drown you, and drive back alone. No one will be the wiser. Everyone will think you've been eaten by the dragon.'

The poor princess had to promise not to contradict the coachman. And as a good princess always keeps her word, her fate was like to be a sorry one.

Grief was turned to gladness in the king's city, when the princess came back alive and well. The king couldn't make enough of the coachman. 'Of course you shall marry my daughter,' said the king, 'and half my kingdom shall be yours. But as the princess is so very young, I think we must put off the wedding for a year.'

The coachman wasn't best pleased when he heard this; but he had to appear satisfied. He was given splendid apartments in the palace, and splendid clothes to wear. A Master of Deportment was summoned to teach the coachman princely manners; and learned counsellors were bidden to instruct him in the duties of princeship. Indeed it was for this very reason that the king had put off the wedding. For though his gratitude to the coachman knew no bounds, he did feel that his dear little daughter deserved a husband who could at least eat his food becomingly.

So the year passed. And at the end of it, the princess said to her father, 'Father, I am still very young. Will you not put off the wedding for another year, that I may grow older and wiser, and more fitted to be a wife?'

And the king agreed to put off the wedding for another year.

The year passed.

At the end of it, the princess went and knelt at her father's feet.

'Oh my father,' she said, 'it may be that I am very foolish, but I do not feel grown up enough yet to take a husband. Have pity on my foolishness, dear father, and put off my wedding for yet one year more. Then I promise you that I will ask no more such favours.'

And the king agreed to put off the wedding for yet a third year.

The third year passed. And the princess wept and said to herself, 'He promised that at the end of three years he would come back. Oh, why doesn't he come?'

But Mario did not come. There was no help for it. The wedding day was fixed; the coachman flaunted about the palace in his princely wedding clothes; and the princess sat and wept over her wedding dress. But put on that dress she must, and go down to the feast she must; for there was to be a grand betrothal feast before the marriage ceremony, and all the people in the town were feasting too, at the king's expense. All the bells in all the steeples were ringing, and ringing, and ringing.

In the midst of all this rejoicing, who should walk into the town but Mario and his three black dogs.

'What is all the feasting and merrymaking for?' he asked. And the the people told him that the princess was to be married to the coachman, who had delivered her from the dragon.

'But the coachman is a liar!' cried Mario. 'It was my dog that killed the dragon! I am going to the palace to tell the king.'

He tried to make his way through the crowds, but they seized him and dragged him before a justice.

The justice frowned on him. And the more Mario protested that the coachman was a liar, the blacker grew the frowns on the face of the justice. And he ordered his constables to take Mario and throw him into prison. So in prison he soon found himself, locked up in a cell with an iron door.

Things were indeed dismal for him! He was lying on the damp floor of his cell, bruised and sore from the rough treatment he had received, and wondering how he would ever escape, when he heard his faithful dogs whining outside the iron door. Then he

knew what he must do, and he leaped up and called out, 'Mustard, good Mustard, come to my rescue!'

In a moment Mustard had bitten a great hole clean through the iron door; and Mario scrambled out through the hole. And there were all the three of his dogs, leaping up to lick his face, and then squatting down and thumping up the dust of the prison courtyard with their black tails.

There was no one in the courtyard – everyone was feasting and making merry. So Mario said, 'O Salt, I am so hungry!' And Salt disappeared, and re-appeared again carrying a napkin full of delicious food. And the napkin was embroidered with a king's crown.

For you must know that Salt had gone to the palace, where the princess sat at the feast in a chair of state beside the coachman. Her arms were dropped at her side, for she had no heart to eat anything. And all of a sudden she felt something wet and warm touching her hand. She looked down and there was Salt, licking her hand, and with a cry of joy she knotted her own napkin round Salt's neck.

'O my father!' she cried. 'He has come back! He has come back!'

'*Who* has come back?' asked the king.

'My deliverer!' said the princess, and she ran round to the king's chair, though the coachman made a grab at her to try and stop her. 'Now I will tell you the whole story,' she said. 'And you will see what a wicked liar the man is whom you have chosen for my husband!'

When the king heard the story, he sent for Mario. The coachman screamed and groaned and begged for mercy. But he was hurried off to prison, and put in the cell, and the iron door was mended up again, so that he could not get out.

Mario took the dragon's teeth out of his pocket and showed them to the king. But there was no need; the king knew he could believe his daughter. Mario took his seat beside the princess, and this time she did not wish for the wedding to be put off. So they were married that very evening.

In the midst of all his happiness and good fortune, Mario thought of his sister, living alone in the poor little house. And he told the princess about her. The princess at once sent a carriage to fetch her, and she soon arrived at the palace, and was given everything her heart could desire – even, by and by, a royal husband, for the king's nephew fell in love with her.

On the morning after this second wedding, the three dogs came to Mario and sat round him in a circle, looking very solemn.

And Mustard opened his mouth and said, 'Master!'

Mario was astonished and said, 'Oh, you can speak!'

'We can speak when there is need,' said Mustard, 'and there is need now. We have come to bid you good-bye. Our work here is done. We have only waited to see that you did not forget your sister in your happiness. And you have not forgotten her. So good-bye, dear Master!'

And, 'Good-bye, dear Master!' said Pepper.

And, 'Good-bye, dear Master!' said Salt.

And when they had said these words, the three black dogs turned into three white birds, and flew away into the sky.

14 · The Dragon of the Well

Once upon a time there was a king who had three daughters. And he called his daughters to him and said, 'My children, I love you better than my life, and I should like to know how much you love me in return.'

Said the first princess, 'Father, I love you like honey.'

And the king was pleased.

Said the second princess, 'Father, I love you like sugar.'

And again the king was pleased.

The youngest princess stood silent. She was thinking deeply. And the king said, 'Come, my little daughter, and how much do you love me?'

'Father,' said the youngest princess at last, 'I love you like salt.'

And the king was angry. 'Salt!' he cried. '*Salt!* A bitter, common thing that the cook takes between finger and thumb and drops into the soup! If you love me no better than that, you are no daughter of mine!' And he took the princess by the arm and hurried her to the palace gate. And there, seeing a poor man passing by, he called to him, and said, 'Here is some unwanted baggage – take her away and marry her!'

The man, whose name was Simonides, took the princess home to his mother, and married her. And they came to love each other dearly, but they were very poor. Sometimes the man had work, and sometimes he hadn't, for the times were hard. And there came a day when they had scarce bread to eat.

Said Simonides, 'Dear wife, if we go on like this we shall presently starve to death. I must journey to the town, and earn some money for the three of us.'

Said the princess, 'Go, my husband, and God go with you.'

So they embraced each other, and Simonides departed.

In the town he met with three merchants who were going on a business journey to the sea port. And he hired himself to them as a servant. And they set out, the merchants riding on their horses, and Simonides on a mule.

The day was hot and the way was dusty, and by and by they thirsted. They drank all the water they carried with them, and still they thirsted. So when they came near to a place where there was a well, one of the merchants said to Simonides, 'Take these four water bottles and go to the well and fill them. We will ride on slowly, and you can catch us up.'

Simonides got off his mule and tied it to a tree, and went to the well with the water bottles. But the well was the home of a dragon, and as soon as Simonides touched the water, the dragon rose up out of it, and he was more hideous to look on than any nightmare.

'Good-day, friend,' said Simonides.

The dragon opened his mouth in a tremendous grin. He was very sensitive about his appearance, and he had never met a man before who had not screamed at the sight of him.

'Since you have called me friend,' he said to Simonides, 'I will not eat you, as I have eaten all the others who came here. Fill your water bottles, friend!'

And he sank down into the well.

Simonides filled the water bottles, and was walking away, when the dragon rose out of the well again.

'Hi, friend!' he called. And his voice was like the beating of a drum.

Simonides stopped and turned round.

'A present for you, friend!' said the dragon. And he gave
Simonides three pomegranates which he was holding in his claws.
'Have you a wife, friend?' he asked.

'I have,' said Simonides. 'The best in the world.'

'Send her one of these pomegranates,' said the dragon with a
grin. 'Keep the other two safely hidden, and do not cut them till
you reach home. A pleasant journey to you, friend!'

Simonides took the pomegranates, and thanked the dragon. The
dragon sank down into the well again; and Simonides fastened the
water bottles to his saddle bow, got on his mule, and rode on after
the merchants.

The merchants grumbled at him for being so long in fetching
the water; but Simonides said nothing. He hid the pomegranates
under his coat; and by and by they met a countryman who was

returning to the village where Simonides lived. And Simonides
gave the countryman one of the pomegranates to take home to the
princess, his wife.

'Tell her I am safe and well,' said Simonides, 'and I hope to see
her soon. In the meantime, I am sending her this little present,
which is all I have to give her.'

The countryman took the pomegranate and went on his way. By
and by he came to the village, and knocked at the door of
Simonides's poor little hut, and gave the pomegranate to the
princess.

'How nice!' said the princess to her mother-in-law. 'We will cut
the pomegranate in two and eat half each. It will refresh us.'

And she got a knife, and cut the pomegranate in two.

'Mother! Mother!' she cried. 'Oh Mother, come and look!'

They could scarcely believe their eyes. They laughed and cried
for joy. For every seed in that pomegranate was a sparkling
diamond.

Now they were rich. They took the diamonds to the town and
sold them, and with the money they built a palace. And at the
palace gate they made a fountain, where all poor thirsty people
might come and drink.

Meanwhile, Simonides travelled on with the merchants, and
when they had done their business at the sea port, they returned
by the way they had come to the town. And there the merchants
paid Simonides his wages, and dismissed him. The wages were
scanty enough, but Simonides took them with great thankfulness.
'Now I have something to buy us food with!' he thought.

And he hurried home to his hut in the village.

But what had become of his hut? It had vanished; and in its place
stood a stately palace, with a fountain sparkling in the sunlight at its
gates. Feeling very bewildered, and no little troubled, Simonides
went into the court of the palace to ask if anyone could tell him

where the princess, his wife, was. And whom should he see, sitting at one of the windows, but the princess herself, dressed in a pretty gown of rainbow-coloured silk. She jumped up and came running out into the courtyard to fling her arms round him.

'Welcome, welcome home, dear husband!' she cried.

'But I don't understand,' said Simonides. 'What has happened? Where *is* our home?'

'This is our home,' said the princess. 'We sold the diamonds you sent, and pulled down the old hut, and built this palace. I hope you like it? Come in and look!'

'Diamonds! *What* diamonds?' said Simonides. 'I sent no diamonds!'

'Oh yes you did,' said the princess. And she told him about the pomegranate, and Simonides said, 'But I have still two more pomegranates!' And they got a knife and cut them open. And in these, also, every seed was a sparkling diamond.

So they sold these diamonds also, and they built an even finer palace, with magnificent gardens. And, remembering how often they had felt hungry, they set up an inn at the gates of the palace, where all poor people might come and eat without paying anything. And they gave away money to all who needed it.

Their fame spread through all the country round. And the king, the princess's father, heard of it.

Said the king to his vizier, 'Who is this stranger who lives like a king, and gives away his money to all who ask? We must pay him a visit.'

And the king sent a courier with a polite letter, asking if he might have the honour of paying Simonides a visit. And the princess sent back a polite letter, inviting the king and the vizier to a banquet. Then she called the head cook and said, 'For today's banquet there must be no salt in any dish.'

'But, my lady,' said the cook, 'the food will be uneatable!'

'Nevertheless, it must be served without salt,' said the princess.

The king and the vizier arrived and sat down to the banquet. The table was laid with gold and silver, and all the dishes looked most tempting. But scarcely had the banquet begun, when the king and the vizier laid down their knives and forks.

'What is the matter?' said the princess.

'You must forgive me, madam,' said the king, 'but I am not hungry.'

'Yet eat a little,' said the princess.

And the king, almost in tears with embarrassment, burst out, 'But there is no salt! And food without salt is uneatable!'

'Oh!' cried the princess. 'And when I told you I loved you like salt, you drove me away!'

Then the king recognized her, and embraced her, and asked her forgiveness. 'I have been foolish and blind,' he said. 'Salt is more needful than sugar, more precious than honey!'

The princess laughed. Said she, 'You drove me away in disgrace, only to find what my heart desired.'

And she clapped her hands and ordered in more dishes, properly seasoned. And they feasted and made merry.

As for the dragon, having found a man to call him friend, he no longer wanted to eat anybody. He allowed travellers to drink at his well, without rising up to frighten them. And sometimes these travellers, when they had quenched their thirst and rested by the well, would drop thank-offerings into the water. These offerings the dragon collected; and were they no more than bent pins or metal buttons, he hoarded them up as his greatest treasures.